"He's dead and I don't want to talk about it!"

Holly's face was streaked with rain and tears. Beneath his hands, Clint felt her body tremble. His face was close to hers. So close… With a groan because he didn't want to, because he knew he couldn't help himself, he pulled her into his arms and kissed her.

The rain came in torrents, but he didn't care because he was holding Holly, kissing her the way he'd wanted to that long-ago summer.

Her body stiffened. "No," she whispered against his mouth, before her body softened.

He kissed her again and again, unmindful of the rain or the force of the wind, kissed her until he went a little crazy. He looked at her through the darkness and the rain. "I don't want this. Lord help me, I don't want…"

Her mouth trembled and he covered it with his and kissed her again. Kissed Holly, his brother's wife.

His brother's widow.

Dear Reader,

Special Edition's lineup for August will definitely make this a memorable summer of romance! Our THAT SPECIAL WOMAN! title for this month is *The Bride Price* by reader favorite Ginna Gray. Wyatt Sommersby has his work cut out for him when he tries to convince the freedom-loving Maggie Muldoon to accept his proposal of marriage.

Concluding the new trilogy MAN, WOMAN AND CHILD this month is *Nobody's Child* by Pat Warren. Don't miss the final installment of this innovative series. Also in August, we have three veteran authors bringing you three wonderful new stories. In *Scarlet Woman* by Barbara Faith, reunited lovers face their past and once again surrender to their passion. *What She Did on Her Summer Vacation* is Tracy Sinclair's story of a young woman on holiday who finds herself an instant nanny to two adorable kids—and the object of a young aristocrat's affections. Ruth Wind's *The Last Chance Ranch* is the emotional story of one woman's second chance at life when she reclaims her child. Finally, August introduces *New York Times* bestseller Ellen Tanner Marsh to Silhouette Special Edition. She brings her popular and unique style to her first story for us, *A Family of Her Own*. This passionate and heartwarming tale is one you won't want to miss.

This summer of love and romance isn't over yet! I hope you enjoy each and every story to come!

Sincerely,

Tara Gavin, Senior Editor

Please address questions and book requests to:
Silhouette Reader Service
U.S.: 3010 Walden Ave., P.O. Box 1325, Buffalo, NY 14269
Canadian: P.O. Box 609, Fort Erie, Ont. L2A 5X3

BARBARA FAITH

SCARLET WOMAN

Silhouette®

SPECIAL EDITION®

Published by Silhouette Books
America's Publisher of Contemporary Romance

To Leslie Wainger,
Con Mucho Cariño

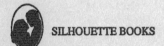 SILHOUETTE BOOKS

ISBN 0-373-09975-4

SCARLET WOMAN

Copyright © 1995 by Barbara Faith

This edition published by arrangement with Harlequin Books S.A.

Printed in U.S.A.

Books by Barbara Faith

BARBARA FAITH

is a true romantic who believes that love is a rare and precious gift. She has an endless fascination with the attraction a man and a woman from different cultures and backgrounds have for each other. She considers herself a good example of such an attraction, because she has been happily married for over twenty years to an ex-matador she met when she lived in Mexico.

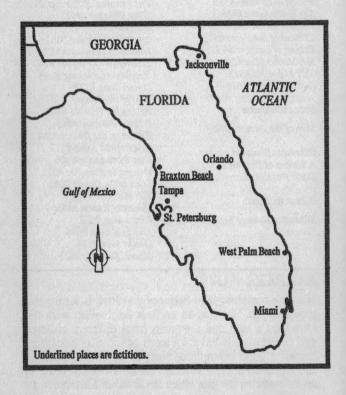

GEORGIA

Jacksonville

FLORIDA

ATLANTIC
OCEAN

Orlando

Braxton Beach

Gulf of Mexico

Tampa

St. Petersburg

West Palm Beach

Miami

N

Underlined places are fictitious.

Chapter One

He sat in the last pew, waiting, wondering if she was going to come. And if she did? What it would be like to see her again. A lot of time had passed. Eight years? Nine? How much had she changed?

He heard muted voices behind him, tensed, then relaxed when an elderly couple started down the aisle and sat two rows in front of him. He glanced around the church, a slight frown creasing his forehead, but he didn't see her.

He hadn't been here in more than a year and he thought as he looked around how much the same everything was. The sun still streamed through the stained-glass windows to cast red and blue and lavender patterns across the polished floor. Bouquets of calla lilies and yellow gladioli graced each side of the altar.

He looked at his watch. Ten forty-four. He heard a rustle of sound and knew without turning that it was her.

She was holding her aunt's arm, walking slowly because the older woman limped. He caught the scent of her perfume, caught only a glimpse of her face when she passed. She wore a simple summer dress; she was still as slim as a reed. As he watched her make her way toward the few remaining seats toward the front, he heard the whispers start.

"It's her!"

"I can't believe she'd have the nerve to show her face."

"You'd think Miss Lou'd have more sense than to bring her here."

He saw her stiffen and hesitate, and knew she had heard. The organ struck the first notes of the opening hymn. She slid into a pew beside her aunt just as the choir came down the aisle, followed by the new minister.

He opened the hymnal, but he didn't sing. He watched her, sitting a little to the side so that he caught a glimpse of her face, the dark cloud of her hair that fell to her shoulders. It seemed to him that even from here he could hear her voice, clear and beautiful, over all of the other parishioners.

Holly Moran. Holly Moran Van Arsdale. Why had she come back? Why was she here?

How many times had she walked down this same aisle with her Aunt Lou? And other times, a few times, with Alan. Sitting in the back of the church so they could hold hands. Never in the Van Arsdale pew with Alan's father or older brother.

Don't let them be here now, she prayed. Please, God.

She had stood here beside Aunt Lou when she was a little girl and she remembered now how hard it had been to be still for an hour. She'd liked the singing, though, especially on the Sundays when her mother sang a solo.

When her mother died her father told her she was singing with the angels. It didn't help. She'd wanted her mother here, not singing "Onward Christian Soldiers" in a long white dress, with wings sprouting out from her shoulders.

She supposed now that whether she liked it or not this church, and yes, Braxton Beach, was still a part of her. A sleepy town with a down-home Southern flavor, thirty miles from Homosassa Springs on the west coast of Florida, a lifetime away from the glitter and glamour of Miami or the bright lights of New Orleans.

"Ring forth the royal diadem..." Over and above the chorus of voices came the shrill off-key squeak of Rose Varnum's soprano. That brought a smile because Rose had been singing off-key for as long as Holly could remember. Whenever anybody mentioned it to Eugene Ferris, the choir director, and said that Rose not only threw the choir off, but the entire congregation, as well, Eugene would sigh and say, "I've tried everything but dynamite. Nothing's going to keep old Rose from singing unless the Lord himself strikes her mute."

They'd even appealed to the Reverend Albert Hendershot, who, according to Aunt Lou, had replied, "Nothin' short of strangling the woman will keep her out of the choir."

Mr. Hendershot had retired four years ago, but in her mind's eye Holly could still see him pounding the pulpit, face flushed almost as red as the suspenders he'd start snapping whenever he got all hot and bothered.

The new minister wore a light gray robe. He had a round, cheery face and spoke in a pleasant well-modulated voice that was far different from Hendershot's raucous bellow. Still, for all the former minister's suspender snapping and shouted threats of hell and damnation, Holly missed him. She had liked him and so had her father. The two men—the hellfire-and-brimstone preacher and the fallen-away Catholic—had been friends and fishing buddies up until Hendershot moved to Fort Lauderdale two years ago.

Her father was a good correspondent and he kept Holly up-to-date on everything that happened in Braxton Beach. He let her know when Mr. Van Arsdale semiretired and when Clint came back from Morocco to take over the running of the Van Arsdale orange groves.

"Clint's doing real good with the business," her father wrote. "He's a lot like old Jonah, tough as a turnip, but he's not nearly as hard on his workers as his father was. Got them putting in an eight-hour day instead of ten and gives them a thirty-minute lunch break, which is something Jonah never did. Last year Clint got himself elected to the state senate and I suppose eventually he'll be a U.S. senator just like his granddaddy was."

The Van Arsdales were rich, politically powerful and socially prominent. They owned orange groves and farming land that ran all the way from Homosassa on over to Kissimmee, to Indian River and Sebring. How it had rankled Jonah when he discovered his youngest son was serious about the daughter of a saloon keeper.

Holly looked up at the pulpit, but she didn't see the minister or the choir or the people around her. Thoughts tumbled around and around in her head, taking her back to that long-ago summer when she was seventeen. Just before Alan went off to Florida State.

His last week at home he'd invited her to the beach party his father gave every Labor Day weekend. She hadn't wanted to go, but he insisted.

"It's my home just as much as it is Clint's and Dad's," he said. "Dad told me to invite my friends. Well, you're one of my friends and I'm inviting you."

The party was held out on the rolling lawn facing the Gulf. To Holly it seemed as though there were almost as many servants as guests. They wandered among the Van Arsdale friends, passing trays filled with fluted glasses of champagne, salty dogs and tequila sunrises. A buffet table was filled with shrimp and crab and Florida lobster, fried chicken, slaw and hush-puppies.

She'd worn a white sundress and high heels and she'd been nervous, unsure of herself. Mr. Van Arsdale greeted her, as he did all his guests, but there had been an expression of cold speculation in his slate gray eyes when he looked her up and down.

For the first half hour Alan stayed right beside her, but when other friends arrived he drifted off. There were a lot of older guests, political friends of Jonah's from Tallahassee, and a few college friends of Clint's, glamorous young women who crowded around him and laughed in beautifully musical trills.

Holly recognized some of Alan's friends, but because Alan had been two years ahead of her at school she didn't really know them. There were two girls who'd just graduated, but they barely acknowledged her. One of them, Betty Ann Higgins, said, "My goodness, what are *you* doing here?" as though Holly had crashed the party.

Stung, Holly turned away and headed for the beach. She left her high heels on the steps leading down and went barefoot to the shore. That's where Clint found her. Though he was only four years older than Alan, he looked much older. He was the serious one, taller, bigger, with dark brooding looks and, even then, a forbidding manner.

"Bored already?" he'd asked.

"No," she said. "No, of course not. It's just that I don't really know anybody except Alan."

"Why aren't you with him?"

"He has other friends." She shrugged. "He's with them."

"Drinking."

She looked at him, then away when a wave washed over her bare feet.

"Do you drink?" he asked.

She shook her head. "I don't like the taste. Besides, my father wouldn't like it."

"Your father owns a saloon," he said as though accusing her of something terrible.

"Yes." She said it with pride. "The Dirty Shame. It's the most popular place on the west side."

His black eyebrows raised half an inch and for a moment the slightest of smiles softened his features. Then he frowned and said, "You still have a year of high school."

"Yes."

"Alan's leaving for Tallahassee on Tuesday."

"I know."

"I hope you'll date other boys while he's gone."

"I wouldn't do that," she said. "Alan and I are going steady. I have his class ring."

He looked at her fingers. "Where?"

She lifted the chain that hung between her breasts. "Here."

His expression changed. He took a step toward her, hesitated, then stopped. "You'd better get back to the party," he said, and turned away.

She didn't see him again until almost midnight when she told Alan she had to get home.

"Party's not over," he said. "How 'bout another dance?"

But when he stood to take her arm he staggered and she knew he was drunk.

"You know I've got a twelve-thirty curfew on weekends," she said. "Please, Alan, I have to go home."

He fished in his pockets, and when he found the keys to his convertible he put his arm around her waist and they started toward the car.

Clint loomed in front of them. "Where do you think you're going?" he asked.

"Going to take my girl home."

"You're drunk."

"No way, bro'. Got a little buzz on. Nothing I can't handle."

Clint took the keys away from him. "Wait here," he ordered Holly, and when Alan protested he took his arm and toe-walked him across the lawn into the house. When he returned he led Holly to his car.

The night was quiet; the air smelled of salt and seaweed. He put a tape in. Something classical. For a long time they didn't speak, but at last he said, "This thing between you and Alan. It isn't any good, you know."

"Thing?" she said, getting angry. *"Thing?"*

"He's going to be away for four years. He'll be seeing other girls."

"No, he won't. Alan and I are in love. We're going to get married."

"My father will never allow it."

"We'll get married, anyway."

He stopped the car in front of her house and turned to look at her. In the light from the street lamp his eyes were the same steel gray as his father's.

She got out of the car. That was the second from the last time she'd seen Clint Van Arsdale.

The minister's sermon—Holly opened her bulletin and saw that his name was Edward Richardson—wasn't anything like the kind of sermons Mr. Hendershot preached. He didn't say anything at all about hell or damnation. When the sermon was over the last hymn was sung and he said the blessing that ended the service.

It was just as hard—no, harder—walking down the aisle. A few people spoke to her aunt, but only one or two said, "Why, Holly Moran, when in the world did you get into town?"

Buford Buckaloo took hold of her hand. He was taller than she remembered, six-three at least, with a lot of belly and a roll of fat under his chin.

"I can't believe it's you," he said. "How long you going to stay?" He ran his thumb across her palm. "Lord-a-mercy, you're even prettier than you were last time I saw you."

That made Phoebe Buckaloo frown. "It's getting late, Buford," she said. "Dinner's waiting. We've got to get home."

"You and Dad go along, Mama." He turned back to Holly. "How about you and me going out for Sunday dinner?"

She withdrew her hand. "I'm sorry, Buford, but I'm afraid Aunt Lou and I have to get home."

"Are you staying with her or at your dad's?"

"With my aunt."

He gave her hand another squeeze and said, "We'll get together soon."

Holly nodded but didn't answer. Taking her aunt's arm she moved toward the entrance. They were almost at the door when she saw Clint. He stepped out of the pew, nodded to her aunt and, when Lou offered her hand, said, "Good morning, Miss Monroe."

"Morning, Clint." Lou hesitated. "Excuse me," she said. "I want to say hello to Mrs. Goode."

He looked at Holly then, not smiling, but offering his hand. "I'd heard you were back," he said.

"Yes." His hand was as cold as his gray eyes. He looked older, taller, broad of shoulder, businesslike and powerful in a dark suit, white shirt, conservative tie.

"When did you get back?"

"Three days ago."

"You live in New Orleans now?"

"Yes."

"Braxton Beach must seem pretty tame by comparison."

"No," she said quickly. "No, it's good to be back." She clutched her purse closer, as though for protection. "How's your father?"

"Dad's fine."

"Well..." She turned, searching for her aunt. "I'd...I'd better go. Aunt Lou's waiting."

He put a hand on her arm, holding her back. The gray eyes challenged, probed. She made as though to move away and he tightened his hand. "I'd like to see you, Holly," he said, his voice low, intense. "Are you at your aunt's?"

Small white teeth fastened on her lower lip. "Yes, but—"

"I'll call you." He let her go and before she could reply he turned away.

She stared after him, trembling, shaken, taking a deep breath to steady herself before she went toward the door to find her aunt.

Aunt Lou introduced her to the Reverend Mr. Richardson, who smiled and said, "I heard you singing. You've got a beautiful voice. I don't know how long you're going to be in Braxton Beach, but I hope you'll consider joining the choir while you're here. We could use a voice like yours."

"My aunt's going into the hospital next week," Holly said. "I'll be busy taking care of her."

"Choir practice is one night a week," Lou put in. "That's not going to interfere with taking care of me or anything else." She offered her hand to the minister. "Holly'll think about it," she said. "Like as not she'll be happy to join the choir."

"Good." He patted Lou's shoulder. "I'll be over some afternoon this week to see how you're doing."

"We'll look forward to it. I've got a nice bottle of sherry waiting to be opened."

He laughed, and to Holly he said, "Choir practice is Wednesday night at seven. Please come."

She smiled because she liked his warm affection toward her aunt. But she didn't say yes because she knew she wouldn't be welcome in the choir. And because she was only going to be in Braxton Beach until her aunt had the surgery and recovered. A month. Maybe a month and a half. Then she'd leave Braxton Beach, this time for good.

* * *

By that afternoon nearly everybody in Braxton Beach knew that Holly Moran, who for a while had been Holly Van Arsdale, was back in town.

It was Phoebe Buckaloo who called Jonah Van Arsdale.

He listened, then stony faced said, "Appreciate your call." When he hung up he looked at Clint and said, "She's come back. That Moran girl is back in Braxton Beach."

Clint looked up from the Sunday paper. "Yes, I know. I saw her at church this morning."

"You know why she's back, don't you?"

"I'd heard her aunt has to have hip surgery."

Jonah snorted. "You think that's the reason?"

"It's the only one I know."

"Then you're a damn fool. She's come back because of the trust fund."

"The trust?" Yes, of course. His father had set up trust funds for both Alan and him when they were children. He'd received his—a million dollars—on his thirtieth birthday. Alan, had he lived, would have been thirty at the end of the year. Was that why Holly had come back? Did she expect, because she was Alan's widow, that the money was rightfully hers? Would she have a legal claim to it?

"After Alan died I had the lawyers structure the fund so that the money would come back into the family," Jonah said. "But maybe there's a loophole. I reckon you better look into it."

"I will."

Jonah began to pace and his face grew red with anger. "She's got no business coming back here looking for money, not after what she's done. You go talk to her, tell her to pack her bags and git.''

"I can't do that.''

"You've got influence, use it!''

Clint stood. ''I doubt she's entitled to anything, but I'll make sure. Believe me, Dad, if she thinks she is she'll have a fight on her hands.''

"Damn right she will! That girl killed my boy.''

"It was an accident.''

"That she caused to happen. She was driving and there was liquor in the car. She killed Alan just as if she held a gun to his head.'' Jonah wiped the sweat off his face with a white handkerchief. Even with the air-conditioning turned to seventy-two, the summer heat and humidity seemed to seep into the room. The fact that he weighed more than three hundred pounds didn't help. Nor did his anger.

"Dammit,'' he roared, ''I don't want that woman here in Braxton Beach.''

"I'll talk to Paul Samuels tomorrow. And don't worry, there's no way in hell that Holly is going to get a cent of Alan's money.''

"See to it.'' With another muttered oath, Jonah turned and stormed out of the room.

Clint walked over to the windows and stood looking out at the Gulf. It stretched for endless miles, flat gray in the afternoon heat, too warm for swimming. Maybe later there'd be a storm to cool things off a bit.

He wasn't sure how he felt about Holly being back in town, but he knew one thing for sure. If his father was right, if she'd come back for Alan's money, she'd have him to deal with.

Memories came then, and this time, as he had so often in the past, he didn't try to push them away.

He had been almost five when Alan was born. It had been a difficult birth, and their mother, a frail woman to begin with, stayed in bed for almost two months afterward. His father was away most of the time and perhaps because she missed him, or because she was afraid and wanted the warmth of someone she loved close by, she insisted on Clint's being with her.

With the baby on one side and Clint on the other she read stories or talked, as though Clint were already grown, of her younger years in Virginia. She told him about trips to Virginia Beach, the cotillions, summer lawn parties and tea dances. In her voice there had been a longing for those girlhood days that had been and were no more.

A year passed, and another, but still his mother didn't regain her strength. When she grew weaker she said, "You'll watch out for Alan, won't you, Clint? Daddy's away so much and even when he's here he's too busy to spend time with us."

She tilted his chin up and with her soft blue eyes looked deeply into his. "Promise me you'll always look after Alan, Clint."

"I promise, Mama," he said. "I promise."

After she died he tried. But looking after Alan hadn't been easy. Alan was a handsome child. From the time he was eight or nine he'd been chased by every little girl in Braxton Beach. When he was sixteen he got a girl pregnant. Jonah, who paid the girl's mother five thousand dollars to send her out of town, had thought it amusing.

"Got a lot of me in him," he bragged. "Damned if I didn't do the same thing when I was his age."

Clint hadn't been amused. He lectured Alan about disease and what the consequences might have been if their father hadn't been wealthy enough to bail him out.

Alan settled down a bit after that. His grades picked up, he made the football team and when he was seventeen he started dating Holly Moran.

By that time Clint was in his junior year at Tulane. When he went back to Braxton Beach for summer vacation his father said, "Alan's taken up with the daughter of the fella who owns the Dirty Shame over on the west side."

"And you don't object?" Clint had asked, surprised.

"Hell, no. Boy's gotta sow his wild oats somewheres. Might as well be with some shanty Irish saloon girl."

"But what if it turns out to be serious?"

Jonah snorted. "It won't. He'll have himself a little fun and when he gets his fill he'll find a nice girl. By the time he goes off to college he'll forget all about Holly Moran."

But Alan hadn't forgotten her.

Clint was surprised the first time he'd seen her because she wasn't at all the way he imagined. With her coal black hair, pale skin and green eyes she was as pretty as an Irish springtime.

He met her at the Labor Day party his father gave just before Alan went off to Florida State. It was funny, but even now he remembered what she wore that day. A white dress and white shoes. He'd watched her and Alan dancing and he knew his father was wrong about her. She wasn't shanty Irish and he'd have bet his last cent she was still a virgin.

He remembered now as he looked out toward the flat gray water that he had followed her down to the beach that day, to set her straight, he told himself. And that later, because Alan had been drinking, he'd driven her home. She had struck him as intelligent and strong-minded and he'd liked her. Even if she was, as his father said, a saloon girl.

The following week both he and Alan went away to school. Alan, being Alan, got into a lot of scrapes that first year and only their father's influence saved him from being kicked out of Florida State.

Clint, busy with his own life, assumed that his brother's romance with Holly had simply dwindled away. But it hadn't. They dated all that summer vacation, and though his father tried to break it up, Alan dug his heels in. He was going to keep on seeing Holly Moran and there wasn't anything his father could do about it.

That fall, supposedly on his way back to Tallahassee, Alan ran off with Holly Moran. They crossed over the Georgia line and got married. And Jonah, as angry as Clint had ever seen him, declared he didn't want anything to do with either one of them.

A year after that, fresh out of Tulane's agricultural master's program, and over his father's objections, Clint took the job with the largest orange grower in Morocco. He'd liked living there, working and learning new ways of growing bigger, sweeter oranges.

He heard from Alan often. Usually in his letters Alan asked for money. And though there was a part of Clint that knew it was time for Alan to grow up and stand on his own feet, he always did what Alan asked. He had promised his mother he would take care of his younger brother; he couldn't let her down.

One day he had a call from his father telling him Alan had been killed in a car crash somewhere down in the Florida Keys. Holly had been driving.

"She killed him," his father sobbed over the phone. "She killed my boy."

Now Holly was back in Braxton Beach.

Clint didn't know how he felt about that. He only knew that if she was after money he'd deal with her. One way or the other.

Chapter Two

Clint called her that Tuesday night. He said, "I'd like to see you. Are you free for dinner tomorrow night?"

A moment or two passed before Holly said, "I ... no. I'm sorry. I'm going to choir practice at the church. Aunt Lou wants me to. I said I would."

"Thursday?" He sounded impatient.

Why did he want to see her? In all the years she'd been away he hadn't tried to contact her. Why now? She tightened her hand around the phone, hesitating while she racked her brain for an excuse. Before she could think of one, he said, "Thursday, then. I'll pick you up at seven."

The phone clicked. She put it down. She didn't want to see him, didn't want to dredge up a lot of old memories. She had known this would happen when she came back, not that she would see Clint, but that memories of how it had been with Alan would come flooding back.

She knew that Clint had asked her to dinner only because he wanted to talk to her about Alan. About the accident. At the thought of it, of how it had been that fateful day, her stomach knotted. She didn't want to open old wounds, to suffer once again the remembered pain of loss.

She picked up the phone, ready to call him back. To tell him that she couldn't go out with him on Thursday night or any other night. But with the phone in her hand she hesitated. What if his father answered? What would she do if she heard Jonah's voice instead of Clint's? She put the phone down.

She'd known when she left New Orleans that this might happen, that sooner or later she would run into either Clint or his father and that they would ask questions. Perhaps, after all, it was better to face it now.

On Friday Aunt Lou was going into the hospital for hip surgery on Saturday. She would see Clint Thursday and, after that, if he asked to see her again, she would be able to tell him that she was occupied caring for Aunt Lou.

She didn't want anything to do with him, yet that night in bed in her old room at Aunt Lou's she kept thinking about him and about Alan. And about that long-ago summer. Yesterday's summer, she told herself. It's in the past, don't think it.

But it was a long time that night before Holly went to sleep, and when she did it was to dream of a tall man with steel gray eyes, and the way she had felt when he looked at her.

On Wednesday night she went to choir practice. She'd been invited by the minister, and if her decision to join the choir was more an act of defiance than of virtue, then so be it.

The Reverend Mr. Richardson welcomed her, and strangely enough so did Rose Varnum, she of the shrieking soprano.

"I remember when you were just a little girl singing in the children's choir," she said. "Sang like an angel and that's what you looked like, too. I'd love for the two of us to sing together next Sunday."

Eugene Ferris gave a strangled cough. "Maybe the Sunday after that, Rose," he said. "I thought it'd be kinda nice if Holly sang a solo next Sunday."

"Well, all right." Rose sighed, but when some of the other members of the choir frowned, she said, "Holly's got the best voice here. Only fittin' she'd sing a solo. Besides, it'd be like we're welcoming her back."

It wasn't much of a welcome. Except for Mrs. Varnum, Mr. Ferris and the minister, no one spoke to her. There were a few mumbles, a nod or two, and the woman next to her actually turned her shoulder away as if afraid of being contaminated.

The choir ran through a few scales and practiced the hymns that would be sung on Sunday. When Holly ran through her solo, "Blest Be the Morn," the other members sat silent and disapproving.

"That was beautiful, Holly," Richardson said when the solo ended. "You're certainly a wonderful addition to the choir."

That brought more frowns and when the practice ended four of the women cornered the minister. As Holly was leaving, she heard one of them say, "You're new here and you don't know anything about her. She's the one run off with the Van Arsdale boy."

"She was driving drunk in the accident that killed him," someone else whispered.

"And she's been singing and God only knows what else down in New Orleans," Phoebe Buckaloo added.

Holly didn't wait to hear Richardson's reply. Aunt Lou's doctor had told Holly that Lou would need care for at least a month after her surgery. She'd stay that long so that she could care for her aunt. After that she'd go back to New Orleans. It was her home; she had friends there. She didn't belong here in Braxton Beach.

Clint arrived a few minutes before seven on Thursday night. Holly met him at the door and, taking her arm, he led her out to his car.

"There's a new place on the beach near Port Richey that I think you'd like," he said. "It's a nice drive so we can talk."

He was quiet as he headed for the beach road. It was a perfect summer's evening, Florida hot but with a breeze off the Gulf and less humidity than usual.

"How do you like living in New Orleans?" he said at last.

"I like it."

"But it's hotter than Florida in the summer."

"You get used to it."

"You're working there?"

"Yes."

"Where?"

"At a club in the French Quarter."

"Oh, one of those," he said.

"What does that mean?"

"I went to New Orleans a couple of years ago. I liked it during my college days at Tulane, but I don't like it now. Especially the Quarter. Porn shops, strip joints, that's all it is."

"No, it isn't," Holly said, bristling. "There are still the good music spots, great jazz."

"Not like it used to be."

"Nothing is."

He looked straight ahead, and in his mind's eye he pictured her singing in some sleazy, smoke-filled bar, drunks propositioning her, pawing her. He swore under his breath and told himself he didn't give a damn what kind of a life she was living. It wasn't any of his business. What was his business, though, was the real reason she'd come back to Braxton Beach.

"I'm surprised you never remarried," he said. "Surely there was someone in your life after Alan." And because he wanted to know, he asked, "Are you seeing someone?"

"I date occasionally."

"Anybody special?"

"No. After Alan..." She shook her head. "There's no one," she said. And, wanting to stop his questions, asked, "What about you? I heard you were married."

"And divorced. Beth lives in Atlanta."

"Any children?"

Clint shook his head. "Too bad you and Alan didn't have a child."

Holly looked down at her hands and it was a moment or two before she said, "Yes, it was."

"I suppose you were too busy..." He hesitated before he said, "Singing."

She wanted to tell him to turn the car around and take her back to Braxton Beach. He didn't like her; he'd never liked her. Why, then, had he invited her to dinner?

They didn't speak after that. He put a cassette on, turned it low and the music of Verdi filled the silence.

"The Triumphal March from *Aida*," Holly murmured.

"You know it?" Clint sounded surprised.

"I majored in music."

"You went to college?" He turned to look at her. "Where?"

"First to Miami-Dade, then the University of Miami, and later in New Orleans. It took six years, but I made it."

"Good for you," he said begrudgingly. "What about Alan? Did he ever finish?"

"No."

"Difficult, I suppose. With a full-time job, I mean."

Holly didn't answer.

The restaurant, an hour's drive from Braxton Beach, was right on the beach. They sat in a glassed-in, air-conditioned terrace overlooking the Gulf. There was no moon. Dark clouds scudded across the sky. Clint ordered a bourbon and branch; she asked for ice tea.

"You're not drinking?"

Holly shook her head. "I've never liked the taste."

He remembered that's what she'd said the night of his father's party, the night Alan had been drunk and he'd taken her home. But it was a lie, of course; she had been drinking the night Alan was killed.

When the waitress returned with the menus, Clint suggested the pompano.

"Then that's what I'll have," Holly said.

"And a Caesar salad?" And again he asked, "You sure you wouldn't like something to drink? White wine, perhaps?"

"No, thank you."

They had little to say to each other after that. Thunder rumbled in the distance. The night grew darker and the smell of rain was in the air. Clint studied Holly while she ate. Her hair, as it had been in church on Sunday, was soft about her face. She had very little makeup on, only a touch of mascara on her thick lashes and a bit of color on her lips. The thought came that she was an uncommonly pretty woman. He remembered that when he had gone to Ireland a few months after his divorce he'd thought about her because she had the same raven black hair and fair complexion of many of the girls he'd seen there.

"Your dad's Irish, isn't he?" he asked. "First generation?"

Holly nodded. "Both of his parents came from County Clare."

"What about your mother?"

"She was born in Georgia. As far as I know from a long line of Georgians. My great-great-great-..." She shook her head. "I don't remember how many greats, but one of them rode in the Civil War alongside of Jeb Stuart. I guess that makes me Southern-Irish."

"Like Scarlett O'Hara," he said.

Her summer dress was the same pale green as her eyes. Her only jewelry was an old-fashioned gold locket that she wore on a thin gold chain around her throat.

He pointed to it. "Pictures?" he asked.

"Yes." She hesitated for a moment, then reached around the back of her neck, unfastened the locket and passed it to him. There was a picture of her mother on one side. "When she was twenty," Holly said. And of Alan on the other side.

His brother at twenty-one or -two smiled up at him with a face so full of youth, of promise and the joy of living that it almost seemed as though he was about to speak. Clint rubbed his thumb across the picture, as if by his touch he could bring Alan closer. "Tell me about him," he said.

Fork poised in midair, Holly looked at him. "What do you want to know?"

"Everything. Anything. What your life was like with him. If he liked living in Miami. If he liked his job."

"He liked it," Holly said with a hint of irony in her voice.

"He was doing public relations, wasn't he? Alan would have been good at that."

"Yes, public relations."

"I've forgotten what kind of a company."

"A rum distillery. One of the big ones that moved to Florida after Castro came into power in Cuba."

"Rum?" Clint grinned. "I bet he could hardly wait to go to work every day."

Holly took a bite of her pampano, but didn't answer.

"Tell me about the day he died."

She bit her bottom lip, and when she tried to pick up her ice tea Clint saw that her hand shook.

"Tell me," he insisted. "Tell me how it was."

"The past is the past," she said in a quiet voice. "Talking about it won't bring Alan back." She laid her napkin on the table. "I really don't want to talk about it."

"He was my kid brother. I have a right to know what happened that day. You were driving, weren't you?"

"Please, Clint—"

"The accident report said no other car was involved. What in the hell happened, Holly? Did you lose control of the car? Go off the road? What?" His gray eyes grew hot with anger. "You were drinking, weren't you?"

"No. No, I—"

"Don't lie to me." In a voice tight with anger, he said, "You were responsible for Alan's death and now you've come back to collect on his trust fund."

"What?" Her voice rose. "What?"

"Don't play the innocent with me. I know all about you. I know—"

She shoved her chair back so hard it tilted and crashed to the floor. Before he could stop her she turned and ran from the room.

He swore under his breath, threw some money on the table and, ignoring the startled faces of the other diners, hurried out of the restaurant. Just as he stepped outside he felt the first spatter of rain, and saw Holly, high heels in one hand, heading down the beach.

"Holly!" he called out, angry at her for running away, angry at himself for having caused her to.

He went after her, thinking how damned ridiculous this was, his chasing a woman down the beach in the rain. He was half tempted to leave her here, let her get back to Braxton Beach any way she could.

Finally, maybe a quarter of a mile from the restaurant, she stopped and stood facing the sea, head down, shoulders hunched, crying. When he reached her, he said her name again. When she didn't answer he put a hand on her arm and turned her so that she would have to look at him.

"Let me go!" she said, and he heard the pain and the anger in her voice.

The wind picked up; the rain came harder. "Come out of the rain," he said.

"No!"

"Look, I'm sorry if I hurt you, but I have a right to know what happened to Alan that day."

"He was killed," she said, her voice rising against the sound of the wind. "That's all, that's it. He's dead and I don't want to talk about it."

Her face was streaked with rain and tears. The pale green dress clung to her slender figure. Thunder rolled and lightning split the sky and he felt her tremble beneath his hands. He looked at her as if he'd never seen her before, and though she struggled to break free he wouldn't let her go. His Italian shoes filled with water; his trouser legs were wet. It didn't matter.

His face was close to hers. So close... With a groan because he didn't want to, because he knew now he couldn't help himself, he pulled her into his arms and kissed her.

The rain came in torrents, but he didn't care because he was holding Holly, kissing her the way he'd wanted to that long-ago summer.

Her body stiffened and she fought him. He wouldn't let her go. He wanted her surrender, her softness. God help him, he wanted her.

"No," she whispered against his mouth. "I don't want this. I don't want..." A shudder ran through her. Her lips softened under his and it was as if when the lightning flashed again it struck through to the very heart of him.

He kissed her again and again, unmindful of the rain or the force of the wind, kissed her until he went a little crazy. He knew he had to stop and so he held her away from him and looked at her through the darkness and the rain. Her hair was seal slick and seal black. Her eyes were wide, her lips were trembling.

He lifted the damp hair off the back of her neck and said, "I don't want this. Lord help me, I don't want..."

Her mouth trembled. He covered it with his and kissed her while the water came up over their feet and their legs, while the thunder crashed and lightning lighted the sky. Holly, his brother's wife. His brother's widow.

Oh, my God! His brother's widow.

He let her go so abruptly she almost fell. "Madness," he said under his breath. And in a voice that shook with all of his inner turmoil said, "This is insane," and started back down the beach toward the restaurant.

Holly stood where she was. She touched the lips still trembling from his kisses. She tried to still the rapid beating of her heart and told herself that he was right, this was insane. It must never, ever happen again.

"Come along," he said in a voice made harsh by all that he was feeling. And when she didn't move he held his hand out and in a gentler voice said, "Come on, Holly. Come out of the rain."

The rain had almost stopped by the time they reached Braxton Beach. They'd said little. He offered her the sweater he had in the back seat, and though she said no, she didn't need it, he'd stopped the car and put it around her shoulders.

When they reached her aunt's house he walked her to the door. "I'm sorry..." He hesitated. Sorry that he had held her in his arms? That he had kissed her? He shook his head as though to clear his thoughts. "You'd better take a hot shower," he said.

She nodded, but didn't look at him.

"When is your aunt going into the hospital?"

"Tomorrow. Her surgery is scheduled for Saturday morning."

"If there's anything I can do..." He took a step closer.

She moved away from him, her back against the door. She took his sweater from around her shoulders and handed it to him. "Good night," she said.

"Good night, Holly. I hope your aunt will be all right." Then quickly, before he could change his mind, he turned and hurried down the steps to his car.

When he reached home he stripped out of his wet clothes and got into the shower. When the hot water hit him he thought about her, about how she was probably in her own shower now, all sweet curves, smooth planes of white skin... His body hardened and he swore under his breath.

When he got out of the shower he dried himself with a towel, then padded barefoot back to his bedroom and got into bed. Don't think about her, he told himself, and tried with every ounce of his willpower not to. But when he closed his eyes he saw her again as she had been tonight in the rain with the green dress plastered tight to her body, showing every curve, the high rise of her breasts... He swore out loud and ordered himself to sleep.

He almost succeeded. He was just rounding the corner of sleep when, unbidden, came the memory of a hot summer's day when Holly was seventeen.

His father had put him in charge of the grove that summer and he still had a week before he went back to Tulane. It was just a few days after the Labor Day party and he'd gone out to see how things were going. It was thirty minutes past quitting time and all of the workers had gone for the day. All except Holly. She was up on a ladder, still picking even though the canvas sack over her shoulder was filled to overflowing. She wore navy blue shorts and a white halter. And she was singing a Randy Travis song.

He thought about the night he'd driven her home after his father's party, the night Alan had been too drunk to drive. Alan had already left for Florida State and he wondered how Holly felt about that. He knew Alan, knew that no matter how crazy his brother might be about Holly, out of sight would be out of mind. But looking at her that day up on the ladder he wasn't so sure Alan would forget her.

He wondered, too, if she and Alan had made love before Alan left for school. Because the thought angered him, he'd called out, more harshly than he intended, "What are you doing here? Quitting time was half an hour ago."

She turned, startled, and lost her footing. He ran forward, arms outstretched, caught her and fell with her. They sprawled under the trees, arms and legs entangled, oranges from her sack spilling out, rolling every which way.

"Oh!" she said, trying to catch her breath. "I'm . . . I'm sorry."

She lay half over him, her halter twisted by the fall, and he could see the smooth skin of her breast peeking through the edge of fabric. Their faces were only inches apart and he felt as though the breath had been knocked out of him. He looked into eyes as green as the leaves of the oranges that lay scattered around them, pale green eyes rimmed with a border of darker green. Her nose was sunburned; she had a sprinkling of freckles across her cheeks.

Even now he remembered the humid scent of her skin, the pungent odor of the oranges, and that for the heartbeat of a moment he felt as though everything had stopped. And that he'd wanted it to.

Her eyes had widened with a strange kind of recognition and he'd felt the rise and fall of her breasts against his chest. What would she do if I touched them? he'd wondered. Would she cry out, move away and scramble to her feet? Or would those green eyes smolder with the same heat that raced through his body? She was so young. On the very brink of womanhood, innocent, waiting. What would it be like to caress this sweet young body, to awaken her to passion? He had been tempted. Oh, so tempted. But then he had remembered she was Alan's girl and he had moved away from her and gotten to his feet. He'd helped her up, and because he'd been afraid that, after all, she might be hurt, he'd driven her home to the gray clapboard house next to the Dirty Shame Saloon.

The neighborhood had been rundown and seedy, and though it was only late afternoon he could hear the loud laughter and music coming through the swinging doors of the bar.

When he opened the car door to help her out, he told her to take a couple of days off. She'd offered her hand and said, "No, I'm all right, really." Strange that even now he remembered how small and cool her hand had felt in his.

That was the last time he'd seen her. During the next summer, a few weeks after her eighteenth birthday, she and Alan had eloped. Now Alan was dead and she had come back to Braxton Beach. Because of her aunt or because of the million-dollar trust fund?

No matter how attracted he might be to her, he was damned well going to find out.

Chapter Three

Aunt Lou went into the hospital on Friday and on Saturday morning she had surgery. Both Holly and her father were there, and though the doctor insisted it wasn't necessary, Holly spent that night at her aunt's bedside.

The next morning the doctor checked Miss Lou and assured Holly everything had gone well. Her aunt, groggy from the anesthesia, insisted that Holly "skedaddle on home and feed the two cats" that were, in cat years, almost as old as she was.

So Holly kissed her aunt and told her she'd be back in a couple of hours.

It was early and the temperature was still in the low eighties when Holly left the hospital. The air was fresh and clean, scented with the sea and summer flowers. She thought, as she walked along the quiet streets, how much she had missed this kind of morning, for while she had adjusted to life in New Orleans she had never gotten used to the moist and smothering humidity of that city. Florida was where she had grown up; it would always be her home. There were so many memories here, good memories as well as bad.

When she started past the library, an old, two-story stone building that had been built in the late 1800s, she paused and went to stand under the shade of a live-oak tree. With a smile she remembered that when she was a little girl she had imagined the library was really a castle. Every time she climbed the stairs it was as if she were entering an enchanted place, for here there were knights and fair ladies, kings and queens, and magical kingdoms where anything was possible.

She had filled her arms with books, her mind with all the wondrous stories they held. Curled up on the window seat in her bedroom or in her bed at night she read book after book, sometimes twice, as if she had a terrible hunger for all they held.

Across the street from the library was the dry-goods store where Aunt Lou bought material to make her school dresses. Next to it was Harold Stentz's music store. It was there that Holly had taken singing lessons from Mrs. Stentz, whose claim to fame was that before her marriage she had sung with the Jacksonville Light Opera Company.

When Holly was fifteen, Miss Mabel said, "I've taught you all I know. You've got a nice enough voice, but you're never going to be an opera singer like I was."

That was perfectly all right with Holly because she'd never had any inclination to sing opera. She wanted to be a singer, all right, but like Billie Holiday or maybe Patsy Cline. She smiled now, remembering, because back then her idea of a singer was of a beautiful and glamorous woman who wore low-cut black dresses, long black gloves, who smoked a cigarette in a long silver holder and who wore a gardenia in her hair just like Billie Holiday. She had visions of herself leaning against a piano singing hot, torchy songs that made people cry.

She didn't wear low-cut black dresses or long black gloves, and the only time she'd tried to smoke she'd almost choked. But she did occasionally lean against a piano, and sometimes her songs made people cry. She wasn't another Billie Holiday, but she had an okay voice and for the past five years she'd been making pretty good money.

When she started past Mrs. Olson's Bakery she hesitated. She'd passed the bakery every morning on her way to grade school. Wonderful smells had wafted from within—bread smells, sweet smells—and sometimes in the winter when it was cold or rainy she'd go in and, looking purposely pitiful, would cast a longing glance at a hot cross bun or a jelly doughnut. "I'm awfully cold, Mrs. Olson," she would say. "Would it be all right if I just stood here for a minute?"

Mrs. Olson always said, "Why, of course, dear. Would you like a jelly doughnut?"

Holly still remembered the first bite into that warm bun, the squirt of jelly on her tongue, licking the powdered sugar off her lips. During her junior and senior years at high school, she worked at the bakery after school. Mrs. Olson had been unfailingly kind and every night before Holly left she'd put two jelly doughnuts in a bag for her to take home.

This morning the smells were just as good as she remembered and, with a smile, Holly opened the door and went in. Mrs. Olson had passed away a year ago and her daughter, Greta, who'd added a coffee bar, ran the shop now. As plump and pretty as her mother had been, Greta greeted Holly with a smile and, without asking, filled a mug with steaming coffee.

"I heard your aunt was in the hospital," she said when she motioned Holly to a chair. "How's she doing?"

"She's still a little groggy from the anesthesia, but she's going to be all right. I'll go back to the hospital just as soon as I have a shower and check on her cats."

"You look tuckered out. You want a hot cross bun or a jelly doughnut? The buns just came out of the oven."

"A jelly doughnut."

Greta served it, then poured a cup of coffee for herself and drew up the chair opposite Holly. "How's it feel to be back?"

Holly took a bite of the doughnut. "Strange."

Greta nodded. "I guess it would. Have you seen the Van Arsdales?"

Holly looked down at her cup. "I saw Clint in church last Sunday."

"He got married, you know. Five years ago." Greta put two teaspoons of sugar into her coffee and stirred. "Beth Anderson. Came from a rich Atlanta family, which suited Jonah Van Arsdale just fine. It didn't work out, though." She looked at Holly. "Clint's an important man in the state now. People say after a couple more years in the state senate he'll run for the United States senate. He'll probably get it, too. Besides being smart he's just about the best-looking man this side of Saint Pete."

"Is he . . ." Holly tried to make her voice casual. "Is he seeing anybody now?"

Greta shook her head. "He dated Lucy Goode for a while, but they broke it off about a year ago. You want more coffee?"

"No, thanks." Holly took the last bite of the dough-nut. "I have to run. How much do I owe you?"

Greta shook her head. "It's on the house. Sort of a welcome home. Mama always liked you, Holly, and so do I. I never believed any of those things people said about you. You come back anytime, okay?"

"I will, Greta. Thanks."

The things people said about her. Thought about her. Like what Clint thought about her.

There had been times, especially in the past few years, when she thought about Clint. Sometimes in the middle of a song, a ballad like "When the World Was Young," with wonderful lyrics about apple trees and youth and memories, she thought not of Alan but of Clint. She remembered that day in the orange grove when they had lain together, when for the heartbeat of a second something magical had happened between them.

She had married Alan; she had loved Alan. Yet in some hidden and secret part of her there were times when she thought about Clint. And remembered.

He was Alan's brother and as far as he was concerned she was still "that saloon girl," the woman who sang in clubs and bars for a living, the woman who had killed his brother.

His mention of Alan's trust fund, his idea that she had come back to claim it, hurt and angered her. She hadn't thought about the fund in years, but now she remembered Alan's talking about it.

"We'll be rolling in dough the day I turn thirty," he'd said. "I'm going to have a million bucks, Holly. We'll be sitting on top of the world."

But Alan hadn't lived to see thirty. He died a week before his twenty-fourth birthday.

She didn't want his money. If she saw Clint again, if he mentioned it, she would tell him she didn't want or need anything from him.

When she left the bakery she went to Aunt Lou's. She fed the two cats, showered and changed clothes, then hurried back to the hospital.

Pat, her father, came in the late afternoon with a bouquet of yellow daisies.

"The worst is over, lass," he said, patting Lou's hand. "You'll feel better tomorrow. I'd have brought you a bottle of sherry if I hadn't been afraid the nurses would throw me out on my ear."

Aunt Lou managed a smile.

They talked a bit and in the early evening he left to go to the Dirty Shame.

It was close to eight when Clint stuck his head in the door. "I hope I'm not intruding," he said when Holly looked up and saw him.

"No... no, of course not." She was too surprised for a moment to say anything else. "Please, come in."

"How's Miss Lou?"

"I hurt like hell." She opened her eyes, looked from him to Holly and raised her right eyebrow. "Good-looking dude," she said and closed her eyes.

He grinned. "How's she doing?" he whispered to Holly.

"The surgery on her hip went well, but she's been in a lot of pain."

"Have you had any dinner?"

"I'll get a sandwich in the coffee shop later."

"You need more than that. Let me take you out somewhere."

"Good idea," Aunt Lou murmured.

And the nurse, coming in with Aunt's Lou's medicine, said, "Your aunt's going to sleep now, Miss Moran. There's no need for you to stay. I'll look in on her from time to time."

Holly hesitated, but when a gentle snore came from the bed she said, "If you're sure..."

"I'm sure." The young woman smiled at Clint. "Miss Moran was here all last night and most of today. Buy her a steak and see that she gets home early."

"Nurse's orders," he said and, taking Holly's arm, led her from the room.

Since the night they'd had dinner on the beach Clint hadn't called or attempted to see her. She wasn't sure now why he'd come to the hospital or why he had asked her to dinner. Braxton Beach was a small town where everybody knew everybody else. He knew who Aunt Lou was, but Holly doubted that he'd ever spoken to her aunt before that Sunday in church.

When they were outside and he led her toward his car, she cast a sideways glance at him. He'd been smiling when he spoke to Aunt Lou, but he wasn't smiling now. His profile in the reflected light in the hospital parking lot was, while not grim, certainly serious.

How unlike Alan he was, she thought, suddenly remembering that long-ago Labor Day party when Clint had followed her down to the beach. She'd been seventeen and he had been ... what? Twenty-three? A serious twenty-three. Solemn and unsmiling even then, but responsible, stepping in when he knew that Alan was too drunk to drive, making sure she got home safely. She'd been a little afraid of him then; she was a little afraid of him now.

They went to the Pelican Inn down on the wharf where the fishing boats came in. There were other boats moored here, small sailboats, motor sailers and cabin cruisers.

"Do you like to sail?" Clint asked when they stopped for a moment to look at the water.

Holly lifted her shoulders. "I don't know, I've never sailed."

"I have a boat. Perhaps you'll go out with me sometime."

Oh? she thought, but didn't say.

They went into the restaurant, and after they'd been seated, Clint said, "You can have that steak if you want it, but the lobster is especially good here."

"Lobster it is, then."

"I tried to phone you at your aunt's. When you didn't answer I came to the hospital. I hope you don't mind."

Holly shook her head. "I don't mind."

She looked tired and he was glad he'd decided to go to the hospital, glad that she was here with him now. He'd meant to offer her an apology for the way he'd acted that night on the beach. He'd planned to tell her that they were, in a way, related. She had been Alan's wife, his sister-in-law, and though there had been no contact between them during these past eight years, now that she was back in Braxton Beach they could, perhaps, be friends. As far as the trust fund was concerned... No, he wouldn't discuss that now. If that was the real reason she had come back to Braxton Beach he'd find it out soon enough.

"How old were you when Alan died?" he asked. "Twenty-two?"

"Yes," she said, looking surprised.

"It must have been difficult for you."

"Yes, it was."

"I've often wondered, why didn't you come back to Braxton Beach?"

Holly hesitated, reluctant to talk about the past, but because he looked at her so intently, waiting for an answer, she said, "Your father objected to our marriage and he didn't want anything to do with Alan after we eloped. That was hard on Alan and I knew it was because of me. Because my father owned a saloon."

He wanted to say that it wasn't true, but he couldn't. If Alan had run away with what Jonah called "the right kind of a girl," his father would still have raised hell. But as soon as he cooled off he would have welcomed the couple back with open arms and a new car for a wedding present. But Alan hadn't married the right kind of a girl; he'd married Holly Moran.

"Maybe things would have been different, eventually I mean, if Alan hadn't been killed," Holly went on. "Maybe he and his father would have reconciled."

"I'm sure they would have," Clint said. And knew even as he said it that, though in time his father might have forgiven Alan, he would never have forgiven Holly. Eight years had passed and none of Jonah's bitterness had lessened.

There was so much he wanted to know about those years before Alan's death, so many questions he wanted to ask. But the questions would wait, now wasn't the time. But one question had to be asked because he'd spent a lot of years thinking about it.

"About the accident," he said. And though he saw the sudden alarm in her eyes and knew she didn't want to talk about it, he went on. "I've never asked you, my father never asked..." He reached across the table and covered her hand with his. "Were you hurt in the accident?"

Her hand trembled beneath his. She pulled it away.
"Yes, I was hurt."

"How badly? Tell me."

"Someday," she said. "Not now."

Their lobster came and for a little while they busied themselves with the food, digging the meat out of the shell, dipping each luscious bite into the warm, melted butter.

"This is wonderful," Holly said. Her tongue came out to lick a smear of butter from the corner of her mouth. He stopped eating and looked at her, wanting to say, "Wait, let me do that." And because that small gesture of hers, that small darting of tongue, had made his body tighten with need, he frowned and stabbed at the lobster as though going after an enemy.

"How many years were you in Morocco?" she asked, breaking in on his thoughts.

"Five years."

"Did you like it?"

Clint nodded. "I love the country. I like the people and the food." He took a sip of the wine he had ordered for himself. "I liked the smell of the place, the color and the excitement of living there. The snake charmers and the camel drivers, the—"

"Belly dancers?" Holly said with a smile.

"You bet." He laughed and before he thought said, "You really should see Morocco. I'd like to take you there someday."

Hot color flooded her cheeks. She said, "Well, I . . . I've always wanted to travel. Perhaps someday . . ." She looked down at her plate, took another bite of the lobster and said, "This really is delicious, isn't it?"

What in the hell was the matter with him, saying he'd like to take her to Morocco? He drained his glass of wine and took another jab at the lobster. And though he didn't want to, he thought of the warm desert nights when the moon had risen over the red city of Marrakesh, and what it would have been like to have spent some of those nights with someone like Holly. And other times, in a bar or a club, watching other men, tourists mostly, dancing with their wives or sweethearts, wishing he'd had someone to hold.

He had liked living in Morocco, but he had felt a loneliness there that he had never known before, a longing for someone to share his life with. Perhaps that was the reason why, when he returned to Florida, he had married Beth.

He had known almost from the beginning that it had been a mistake. They were ill-matched; they didn't get along. He wanted children; she didn't. His idea of a vacation was at a resort somewhere on the beach; hers was a shopping trip to New York. He had tried and so had she, but it hadn't worked out. His finding out about her affair with the golf pro had been the final straw.

He and Holly had little to say to each other after that, except to discuss whether they should order chocolate crepes or apple pie, regular coffee or decaf. When they finished, after having decided on the pie, Clint asked for the check.

He took her arm when they left the restaurant. The air smelled of saltwater and fish. Some of the boats were strung with lights that reflected onto the water; a few voices floated on the night air.

"Would you like to take a look at my boat?" Clint asked.

"All right."

They walked out onto the pier. His boat, a forty-foot motor sailer, he told her, was in a slip at the end. "Here she is," he said.

"*Straight on Till Morning,*" Holly said, reading the name on the bow. "That's nice. Peter Pan?"

He nodded, looking pleased. "The way to Neverland. Second star on the right. Straight on till morning." He took Holly's hand. "Come have a look at her."

The boat rocked gently when they stepped aboard. He led her around the deck, said, "Careful," and helped her down the three steps to the cabin below.

The galley was equipped with a small refrigerator, a two-burner stove and a microwave. There was a built-in nook with a table big enough for two, maybe four if they squeezed in close. Beyond the galley there was a lounge with one easy chair, two captain's chairs, padded benches and built-in shelves against each side.

"The bedroom's through here," Clint said, motioning Holly through a doorway at the end of the lounge. There was a built-in bunk that was a little wider than a single bed. On the shelf above the bunk there were a few books—Tom Clancy, John Grisham, a book on sailing, one on the history of the Keys and Key West and the complete works of Robert Service.

"A bunch of the boys were whooping it up in the Malamute saloon," Holly said with a smile, quoting from "The Shooting of Dan McGrew."

"You know it?" he said, sounding surprised.

"My dad loves to recite it when he's had a nip or two of the Irish."

Clint laughed. "I don't know your father," he said. "I've seen him around, of course, but I don't think we've ever spoken. I've never been in his place."

"The Dirty Shame."

"Funny name."

"Yes, I guess it is."

They looked at each other and suddenly she became aware that they were alone, standing close together because of the confines of the cabin. She looked down at the narrow bed, stepped back, or tried to, just as a wave rocked the boat. She stumbled and Clint reached out to steady her. "Damn speedboats," he muttered.

The boat rocked again, jostling her against him. He put his arms around her. "Happens every time one of those hotshots speeds past the pier. They've been warned about it, but they have a few drinks and think they own the—" He stopped and looked down at her. He said, "Holly?" and as though afraid she might escape he tightened his arms around her.

"I'm . . . I'm all right now. You can let go of me."

"Of course." But he didn't let go. He held her there, looking at her, puzzled by all of the emotions he suddenly felt.

"Clint?"

He shook his head, and before she could speak again he covered her mouth with his. He told himself he hadn't meant this to happen, that it wasn't why he had brought her aboard. He would let her go in a moment. But, oh, how sweet her mouth was. And the feel of her, of that slender body pressed close to his.

He felt her resistance, then the slight softening, and heard her sigh when her lips parted under his. He thought of all the nights he had spent alone on his boat, and knew what they would have been like if she had been with him. If they had lain together on his bed and felt the gentle roll of waves beneath them.

His body hardened with need. He put his hand against the small of her back and urged her closer. She murmured a protest, then with a gasp she swayed against him. For a moment. Then she stepped away.

"No," she whispered. "Please, no."

He released her. "Sorry," he said, stepping back as much as he could in the small place, bracing one arm against the bulkhead. "This isn't why I asked you to see the boat."

"I know." She ducked under his arm and headed into the saloon. "I want to be at the hospital early tomorrow," she said, sounding breathless. "I really have to go now."

"I'm sorry, Holly. I didn't mean . . ." He ran a hand through his hair. "Blame it on the wine."

"Or the speedboat," she said, offering a smile.

He felt some of the tension ebb and, smiling back, he took her arm to help her up the steps to the deck. Once there, Holly stopped and looked out over the water. "I like your boat," she said. "Thank you for showing her to me."

"Anytime." But even as he said the words, Clint knew there wouldn't be a next time. Being alone with Holly was too dangerous; he had to make sure it didn't happen again.

He drove her home and walked her to her door. He made no attempt to kiss her. Instead, he said a hasty good-night and hurried to his car.

The following day when her father came to the hospital he said, "Murphy O'Brien's wife called this morning. Seems Murph had a couple of drinks after the couple of drinks he'd already had before he left the bar last night. When he got home he had a few more. Fell down the basement stairs and sprained both his ankles."

"That's terrible!" Holly said.

"Yes, 'tis. Though between you and me and Aunt Lou I wouldn't be a'tall surprised if Mollie hadn't pushed him down. She's been threatenin' to do something like that for years. Maybe she found her chance."

"Shame on you, Patrick Moran," Aunt Lou said. "Mollie O'Brien is a good woman."

"Too good for the likes of old Murph." He patted Lou's shoulder, and to Holly he said, "I been thinkin', darlin', that maybe you could help me out while Murph's laid up."

"But what about Aunt Lou? She'll be out of the hospital soon. I don't want to leave her alone."

"It's only on weekends I'd be wantin' you."

"Hattie'll be glad to stay evenings," Aunt Lou said, referring to the twice-a-week cleaning lady she'd had for the past twenty years. "She could use the extra money."

"I really need you, Holly dear," Pat said.

"Well . . ." But before she could say anything else her father hugged her. "Done and done," he said.

The nurse came in then with a pair of crutches. In her middle fifties, almost six feet tall, with bosoms that preceded her by at least eight or nine inches, and a wild mop of hair as red as Pat's, she approached the bed.

"Time to get up and start moving, Miss Lou." The way she said it meant this wasn't a request but an order.

She took the pillow from between Lou's legs, handed the crutches to Pat, then helped Aunt Lou sit up and put her legs over the side of the bed. Gripping her patient under the arms, she ordered, "Now stand."

Aunt Lou looked terrified. "I hurt," she said, moaning in pain. But there was little she could do against the redhead who motioned to Pat for the crutches and stuck them under Aunt Lou's arms.

With her arm around Aunt Lou, she helped her to the door and into the hall.

"The woman's a harridan." Holly looked upset. "Poor Aunt Lou is in pain. She can barely move, let alone walk." She went to the door and peered out. Her aunt, though grunting in pain and barely able to move, was somehow managing a few steps.

They were only gone five minutes, and when they came back into the room the nurse helped Aunt Lou back to bed. "The therapist will be in later," she told her patient. "You can rest until she comes." She looked at Pat and Holly. "It's better if the two of you leave for a while," she said. Once again it wasn't a suggestion, it was an order.

"Very well, Miss..." Holly hesitated. "I'm sorry, but I don't know your name."

"O'Toole."

"O'Toole, is it?" Pat smiled. "I'm Moran. Patrick Moran."

"Uh-huh," the nurse said.

"Have you ever been in my pub? The Dirty Shame?"

"No," she said. "And that's a dirty shame."

Pat laughed. "It'd be nice if you did. You and... ?" He raised a questioning eyebrow. "Is there a Mr. O'Toole?"

"Not anymore."

"Ah." Like a mischievous leprechaun, Pat's smile widened and his blue eyes twinkled. "Why don't you come over this Saturday night, Miss O'Toole? I'll see that you're taken home."

"I'll think about it," Nurse O'Toole said. And with her bosoms leading the way, she marched out of the room.

Holly stared at her father. As far as she knew he hadn't been interested in a woman since her mother died. Yet he'd looked at the tall, red-haired nurse as though she was the answer to his prayers, as if he'd been hit over the head with a two-by-four.

"What a darlin' girl," he said. "I can hardly wait till Saturday night."

That night, weary from the long day and evening at her aunt's bedside, Holly went to bed with a book. She had just started reading when the phone rang.

"It's Clint," he said when she answered. "Did I wake you?"

"No, I was reading."

"I tried to call earlier."

"I've been at the hospital most of the day."

"How's your aunt?"

"She's better, but still in a lot of pain."

"I'm sorry."

"I had a nice time last night, Clint," she said. "Thank you for dinner."

"My pleasure." He cleared his throat. "I've been thinking," he said. "About the trust fund. If you want to—"

"The trust fund?" She sat up straighter in bed, frowning at the phone.

"If you want to talk about it with an attorney you can, of course. But I thought we might find a more simple solution. Perhaps a settlement can be worked out so that we can avoid any lengthy litigation."

She wasn't sure what she'd expected when she heard Clint's voice, but she hadn't been prepared for this businesslike talk of trust funds and settlements.

"Holly?"

She took a deep breath and said, "I don't want a settlement, Clint."

"I see." His voice hardened. "Well, let me tell you right now that if you expect—"

"I don't expect anything." She cut him off. "I don't want anything."

"Only a million dollars, right?"

Holly glared at the phone. "Wrong," she said. And hung up.

In a few minutes the phone rang again. She let it ring. Last night Clint had held her in his arms. He had kissed her with warmth and passion. How could he believe that the only reason she had come back to Braxton Beach was to get a share of Alan's money?

Just for a moment she wondered if maybe she should see a lawyer. After all, she was Alan's widow. He'd taken so much from her, maybe it was her turn to get something back.

But even as the thought came, she pushed it away. She didn't want the Van Arsdale money. And she certainly, by God, didn't want or need another Van Arsdale in her life.

She reached up and snapped the light off, not quite sure why she'd started to cry.

Chapter Four

Holly liked being back at the Dirty Shame. Everything was familiar to her here—the smell of beer, hot coffee topped with good Irish whiskey and a dollop of cream, the pretzel machine and the crock of melting cheese to dip the pretzels in, the bowls of potato chips and peanuts and hot salty french fries. It was good to hear the voices of convivial people when they gathered around the rinky-dink piano to sing old Irish songs and tell old Irish jokes.

These were the people from the neighborhood where she had grown up—the Raffertys and the Kellys, the O'Reillys and the Cohans, the Simoskis and the Cantinis, the Gomezes and the Muellers.

Bald and skinny Jimmy Collins, who had been the piano player for as long as she could remember, still played six nights a week. That night as soon as Holly walked

through the swinging doors he struck a chord and started
to play "My Wild Irish Rose."

And her dad, spiffy in a green bow tie and green suspenders, said, "Welcome back, lass. We've missed you."

Mrs. Rafferty hugged her and old Mr. Cantini, who
at ninety-two still had a wicked gleam in his eye, kissed
both her cheeks.

She served beer and Irish, filled bowls with potato
chips, peanuts and french fries. And when later in the
evening some of the customers gathered around the piano to sing, and they called out to her, "Come join us,
Holly," she stood with them and sang "The Boys from
County Cork," a song she'd learned in her childhood.

She stayed until two o'clock closing time that Friday
night and it was after three by the time she got to bed.
The next morning she slept until almost ten and, when
she saw the time, hurried out of bed and into the shower.

She fed the two cats and laughed when they twisted
themselves around her ankles, purring in unison, me-
owing for her to hurry. She liked this old-fashioned
kitchen and enjoyed puttering in it. There was a fireplace at one end of the room and she had lovely memories of cold spells when Aunt Lou would build a fire
before she started their breakfast. Sometimes, if it was
very cold in the kitchen, the two of them would heap
their plates with bacon and eggs and sit by the fire, she
on a low stool, Aunt Lou in her rocking chair, the two
cats curled up close by.

But it was summer now and the sun streamed in
through the blue-and-white checkered curtains. Holly
hummed to herself as she set a place at the counter bar.

Barefoot, wearing only shorts and an oversize shirt,
she put the coffee on and took a box of cereal out of the

cupboard. The coffee had just started to perk when Buford Buckaloo knocked at the screen door.

"Morning," he called out. "How you doing? How's your Aunt Lou? I just came by to ask about her."

"She's doing all right." Holly hesitated and, because it seemed unfriendly not to, opened the screen door and asked, "Would you like a cup of coffee?"

"Sure would." When he came in he looked her up and down, starting at the bare legs, traveling over her body, staring at the loose shirt under which she hadn't bothered to put a bra. "You're a sight for a hungry man's eyes," he said. "Do you always look this good in the morning?"

She poured his coffee without answering him, put the cup on the counter bar and wished she hadn't invited him in.

"Heard you were back helping your dad," he said. "Must be quite a comedown after New Orleans." He pronounced it Noo Orleens.

"I like working in my dad's place." Holly glanced at the wall clock. "I'm going to go to the hospital as soon as I finish breakfast."

"How 'bout you and me having dinner tonight?"

"Sorry, but I'll be working."

Buford put his cup down. "Tomorrow night?"

"I'm afraid not."

"Aw, c'mon, Holly. I got a hunch you 'n' me could make some nice music together."

"Not any kind of music, Buford."

He laughed and before Holly could move he came around the counter toward her. She said, "Back off, Buford."

Grinning, he made a grab for her. She tried to dodge out of his way but he captured her hands and pulled her up against him. "Don't play games with me," he said as he pressed her back against the counter.

"Damn you, Buford, let go of me!" She struggled to get away from him, but before she could turn away, he covered her mouth with his.

"Let me go!" she said, and freeing one hand pushed hard against his chest. He swore at her and his face twisted with anger. When he tried to grab her again she screamed.

The screen door flew open. Clint ran across the room. With a roar he grabbed Buford by his shirt collar and whipped him around.

Buford, taken by surprise, staggered back. "What...?" he managed to say. "What the hell...?"

Clint grabbed him by the scruff of his neck, said, "Open the door," and when Holly did he heaved Buford Buckaloo out the door, down the steps and onto the grass. "You come back here again and you'll be in traction for a month," he yelled to Buckaloo.

He slammed the door shut and, turning to Holly, gripped her shoulders and said, "Are you all right? Did he hurt you?"

"No." She tried to catch her breath. "No, I...I'm all right. I shouldn't have let him in. I told him to leave, but he...he grabbed me and I couldn't..."

Her teeth were chattering and her face was pale. Clint put his arms around her and before she could say anything else he picked her up and carried her to the rocking chair.

"What...what are you doing?"

Without answering he sat down and pulled her up onto his lap. When she struggled he said, "I just want to hold you for a minute."

She pushed against his chest, but he wouldn't let her go. He put one hand against the back of her head and pressed her close, holding her, soothing her, whispering that it was all right, everything was all right because he was here and nothing was going to hurt her.

Little by little she began to relax and stopped trying to move away from him. He felt warm and good and solid and she knew she was safe here in his arms. She closed her eyes and curled her legs up against him. He held her like that, held her and rocked her and warmed her. He patted her bottom as though she were a child and kissed the side of her cheek.

She told herself she would only stay like this for a minute, but then she turned her head into Clint's shoulder and smelled the good man smell of freshly laundered shirt and clean skin. And stayed as she was, letting him hold her and rock her.

"The coffee's perking," she said at last.

"Let it perk. Why did you let Buckaloo in?"

"He said he'd come to ask about Aunt Lou. I thought it would be all right. I didn't know he was like that."

"I don't think he'll bother you again."

She made as though to get up then, but he tightened his arms around her because he didn't want to let her go. It was good to sit here with her like this in this old-fashioned kitchen with the smell of coffee perking on the stove and the two cats curled up in a patch of sunlight. How different this was from the big steel-and-chrome kitchen in his father's house. He'd never had breakfast there, not even when he was a child. Their kitchen had none of the warmth of this pleasant room. It didn't invite you to pull up a chair and have a cup of coffee.

He'd always thought of this section of Braxton Beach as the poor side of town, the place where the Irish and the Poles, the Italians and the Cubans, lived. Did other families have kitchens like this? Did husbands and wives and children gather around a big round table like the one in this room? Was there chatter and nonsense, laughter and jokes? Was there warmth and love and caring?

Perhaps his own growing-up years would have been different if his mother had lived. Perhaps his father wouldn't have been so cold, so distant. No wonder Alan had sought out a girl like Holly; he'd been looking for the love he'd never gotten at home.

Now Alan was dead, and his wife, his widow, lay cradled in Clint's arms. If that caused a feeling of guilt and betrayal, he pushed it away. Her skin was soft and fragrant. She was so feminine and somehow so fragile. He wanted to keep her close to him like this forever.

He said, "Holly?" and when she turned her face up to his, he kissed her. It was a quiet kiss, a gentle kiss. He moved his lips against hers, and though at first she did not answer him, she didn't move away. Then slowly her arms crept up around his neck and her lips softened under his.

He held himself back, content to feel her close, to kiss the lips so sweetly parted for him. He kissed her like that for a long time, but soon the need to touch her grew and when it did he unfastened the first two buttons of her too-big shirt and began to stroke her breasts. She stiffened. She said, "No, you shouldn't."

But the skin of her breast was like satin against his fingers, soft, so unbelievably soft. For a little while everything was forgotten. There were only the tender kisses, the gentle touchings.

As though from afar Holly heard the squeak of the rocking chair and the perking of the coffee on the stove. She knew she should move, but instead she leaned closer, content to stay like this with him, to answer his kisses, to feel the touch of his fingers against her skin.

But at last, when she felt his body tighten, when the breath came fast in her throat, she said, "Clint? Clint, we've . . . we've got to stop."

"I know." His voice hoarse against her lips. "I know." He took a deep breath and loosened the arms that had held her so tightly. He smoothed the hair from her face, kissed her cheek and said, "I didn't mean for this to happen."

"I know." She slid off his lap.

He got up and, going to the stove, turned the fire off under the coffee and filled two cups. Taking her hand he led her to the table. She sat across from him. Her hair was tumbled about her face; her lips were swollen from his kisses. She pulled her shirt closer around her and tied it at her waist, but he could see the outline of her breasts, the push of the still-aroused nipples against the fabric.

He gripped the cup and hoped she wouldn't notice that his hands were shaking. "I came here this morning to apologize for what I said last night on the phone. About the trust fund, I mean."

She looked down at her coffee.

"Did you know about it?"

"Yes, Alan told me. He said when he turned thirty he'd have a lot of money."

"A million dollars." Clint stirred his coffee. He hated to talk about this, but knew he had to. "After Alan died my father fixed it so that you wouldn't be able to touch the trust. I agreed with him at the time, but I'm not so sure I do now. You're Alan's widow. You're entitled to at least a portion of the trust."

Holly set her cup down. "You don't understand," she said. "I don't want the money, Clint. I don't want anything from your father or from—"

"From me?" he asked. And when she didn't answer, he said, "You know, it's strange, Holly, but in spite of everything that's happened over the years, your running away with Alan, the accident, his death..." He paused and shook his head. "Even when I blamed you for what happened to him I couldn't stop thinking about you. There was a part of me that hated you..." He stopped, unable to go on.

"Because I was alive and Alan was dead," she said.

"I know how wrong that was. I know it was an accident. The weather was bad. It wasn't your fault..." He hesitated because he wanted to say, Was it? Could you have avoided the accident? Had you been drinking?

Instead he said, "All the old, angry memories came back when I heard you'd returned to Braxton Beach. But at the same time the thought of your being here excited me. You were my brother's wife, it wasn't right that I felt the way I did." He reached for her hand. "The way I do. It seems almost..." He shook his head, loath to say the word.

"Incestuous," she said.

"Yes." He took a deep breath and, getting up, crossed the room and stood with his back to the fireplace. "There are still so many things unresolved in my mind," he said.

"About the accident."

"And the way I feel about you. I'm attracted to you, Holly. I think I have been since that long-ago day at my father's party. And that afternoon in the grove when you fell into my arms." He looked at her; his face was tortured by all of the conflicting emotions churning inside him. "But there's so much that stands between us," he said. "You were Alan's wife. You loved him, you slept with him..." He turned so that his back was toward her and leaned both hands on the fireplace. "Alan will always stand between us," he said.

She wanted to go to him, wanted to put her arms around him and say, There are so many things you don't know about Alan, so many things you don't understand. But she didn't. She only sat there, waiting. When at last he turned away from the fireplace, the warmth she had seen in his eyes when he had held her had faded to a gray coldness.

He said, "Would you like me to wait and drive you to the hospital?"

"No, thank you," she managed to say. "I . . . I like to walk."

He went to the door. "I don't think Buford will be back, but just in case you'd better keep this locked." He opened the door, then the screen. But still he hesitated. "Think over what I've said about the trust fund," he said. "My father's a tough man to deal with, especially when he's as angry as he is about this. About you. But perhaps something can be worked out. If you'll agree to a settlement—"

"I don't want Alan's money," Holly said tightly. "I've told you, Clint. I don't want anything."

He looked at her and she knew by the expression she saw in his eyes that he didn't believe her.

"Goodbye," he said. Then he went out and she stood there in the middle of the kitchen.

She had been alone many times in her life, but she'd never felt this particular kind of aloneness. It was as though all of the sunshine had gone out of the room. As though a part of her life had just stepped through the door.

The Dirty Shame was so crowded and busy that night that Holly had little time to think about Clint. In addition to the regulars, Greta Olson was there, accompanied by a tall, good-looking man in his early fifties.

Greta introduced him. He'd just moved to Braxton Beach from Ocala. They'd been dating for three months, Greta said and, with a blush, whispered, "We're getting married in August."

Holly congratulated them; her boyfriend beamed, then ordered a pitcher of beer. When Holly brought it to their table, along with a bowl of hot french fries and chips, she said, "Tonight is on me, so enjoy."

When, an hour later, Holly paused long enough to take a deep breath, she became aware that her father kept looking toward the door. He was very handsome tonight with his hair slicked down, a new white shirt and a red bow tie. He laughed with his patrons, told as many jokes as they did, but he seemed nervous and kept his eye on the door.

It was a little after ten when Nurse O'Toole arrived. Pat, with all the vigor of a teenager, vaulted over the bar and hurried to her. "There you are," he called out when he reached her. "I was afraid you weren't coming."

She looked around the room. "Noisy," she declared, "but I like the looks of it."

Pat took her arm. "I could make somebody move and give you a table," he said, "but I was hoping you wouldn't mind sitting at the bar so we could talk."

"The bar's fine. You have any Irish whiskey?"

"As much as you can drink, darlin'." He led her to an empty stool at the end of the bar. All night long somebody or other had tried to sit there. But Pat had kept shooing people away, saying, "I'm expectin' someone." Now that someone was here.

Holly came over to say hello. Nurse O'Toole said, "Your aunt's fine and anxious to go home tomorrow. Have you got somebody there to take care of her?"

"I'm staying with her. When I'm not there Hattie Hellinger will be."

"I know Hattie. She's a good woman, strong as an ox." O'Toole took a sip of her Irish over ice and said, "Your aunt will have to come in for therapy twice a week. When she's home she'll need to keep walking because for a while it'll be like learning all over again. Sitting will be uncomfortable, so get her up as much as you can."

"I will," Holly said, knowing that if she didn't and the nurse found out about it she'd raise hell with her.

"Your dad's a real good-looking man," O'Toole said.

"Yes, I... I guess he is."

"Been widowed long?"

"Almost twenty-one years."

"Too long," the nurse said.

Holly wasn't sure how she felt about that. She was happy that her dad was happy. But Miss O'Toole? The woman was built like a two-ton truck. She had the personality of spiked shoes and a voice like a circus barker with hemorrhoids. The idea of her as a stepmother made Holly want to catch the first bus back to New Orleans.

But a little while later when she looked down toward the end of the bar she saw her father and the nurse with their heads bent toward each other. There was a twinkle in Pat's eye and a surprisingly soft expression on O'Toole's face. In spite of herself, Holly smiled. It was an unlikely match, but who was to say what drew two people together?

That made her think of Clint. Even above the chatter, the laughter and the music she thought about him. What manner of man was he? He could be tender; he could be as kind as he had been today when he'd held and rocked her. But he could be cruel, too.

It hurt more than she would ever have thought it would to know that he thought she had come back because of Alan's trust fund. He didn't trust her, yet she knew he was attracted to her. As she was to him. That was something neither of them could deny. She had known it that night on the beach when he kissed her with such anger, such passion. When they'd kissed on his boat. And this morning when he held and rocked her. She had sensed it that long-ago summer's day when she'd fallen into his arms from the orange tree.

But she must not give in to her feelings because Clint was as wrong for her as Alan had been. And God knows, one Van Arsdale was enough to last a lifetime.

With a sigh, Holly picked up her empty tray and headed back to the bar. That's when she saw him.

The place was too noisy, too crowded. He didn't know why he'd come. Then over the heads of the customers he saw Holly, and knew.

She came toward him, wearing a simple white blouse and a black skirt. She said, "I didn't know you were coming."

"I thought it was time I checked the place out."

"I see." She offered a tentative smile. "Would you like a table or do you want to sit at the bar?"

"A table, please."

It wasn't what he expected, he thought as he followed Holly to a corner table. Most of the people here were older couples, husbands and wives out together on a Saturday night. The only single women seemed to be a table of five, all in their seventies and eighties, having a whale of a time.

When he was seated, Holly said, "What would you like?"

"A beer will be fine." And before she could move away he said, "What time are you through?"

"We close at two."

"May I take you home then?"

She hesitated. Before she could answer a customer called out, "Another pitcher of beer, Holly darlin'," and she turned away.

He rarely came to this part of town. The last time he had been here he'd been campaigning for the state senate. The place wasn't as bad as he'd thought it would be. On the other hand it was a hundred years removed from either the Braxton Beach Country Club or the Palm Beach Club. Still, in a quaint sort of way it was rather pleasant. A crowd of men and women were gathered around the piano, a few of the older couples were dancing. Nobody seemed to be drunk; everybody was having a good time.

Holly made her way back toward him. She took a pitcher of beer off her tray and put in on the table where the five single women were, then brought him his beer and a plate of hot french fries.

"Is there anything else?" she asked, raising her voice because the people gathered around the piano were singing "When Irish Eyes Are Smiling."

"No," Clint said. "I..." But just then one of the group around the piano called out, "Holly! Come give us a song, girl."

And when she shook her head, one of the men left the group and came toward her. "Come on," he said, taking her arm. "It's been a month of Sundays since we've heard you sing."

She looked at Clint. He said, "I don't know how anybody can hear you over the noise."

The group around the piano moved aside. Someone said, "Can you be singing "Danny Boy" for us?"

The piano player struck a cord and said something to Holly. She nodded and began to sing. As though by a signal the room grew quiet.

Her voice, so clear and sweet, so rightly Irish, drifted through the room like cool wine into crystal. The smoke-filled bar faded and in his mind's eye Clint saw the green fields of Ireland. The words of love and loss, of nostalgia for days that had been and were no more, washed over him and suddenly, unbidden, came the thought of his brother, not as he was when he had last seen him, but as a child, a boy with buttercup hair who followed him everywhere, calling, "Wait for me, Clint. Wait for me."

He thought of his dead mother, too, and remembered the long afternoons when he sat beside her on the bed, and of the promise he had made her that he would always take care of Alan.

He thought of his broken marriage and knew that much of it was his fault because he hadn't been able to give Beth the love she'd needed. Because there was a coldness inside him, an unwillingness or fear to either give or receive love. He wished it was not so, but knew that it was.

Everyone else in the room faded, and there was only Holly in her simple white blouse and black skirt, with the dark cloud of hair about her face. She looked toward him and for a moment it was as if she was singing just to him.

"Oh, Danny Boy...oh, Danny Boy, I love you so...."

The song ended with a wild burst of applause.

But Clint didn't applaud. He only sat there, looking at Holly. And wondering why his eyes stung with unshed tears.

Chapter Five

"What're the likes of him doin' here?" Pat asked when he spotted Clint at the table in the corner.

"I don't know." Holly poured peanuts into a bowl. "He came by Aunt Lou's this morning."

"What in the devil for?"

"To talk about Alan." She hadn't told her father about Buford's visit, but now, because he was looking at Clint as though any minute he was going to order him right back out of the swinging doors, she said, "Buford Buckaloo was there when Clint arrived. Buford grabbed me and he was..." She hesitated, reluctant to tell Pat, but wanting him to know that if it hadn't been for Clint she'd have been in real trouble. "Clint heard me call out. If it hadn't been for him—"

"That Buckaloo bastard!" Pat whipped off his apron, grabbed his cap and headed for the door. Holly stopped him. "Clint took care of him," she said.

"Knocked his block off?"

"Threw him down the back steps."

"Well, then . . ." Pat gave her a hard look. "But you know how I feel about the Van Arsdales?"

"Yes, I know."

"On the other hand he helped you out when you needed it. I won't ask him to leave, but I'm tellin' you right out, don't go gettin' mixed up with him."

"I don't intend to."

When the hour grew late and most of the crowd cleared out, Clint moved to the bar. Holly introduced the two men. Pat shook Clint's hand, fixed him with his steely blue eyes and said, "My daughter tells me you threw Buckaloo out of her house this morning."

"He deserved throwing out."

Pat indicated a stool next to the nurse. "Rosie," he said, "this is Mr. Van Arsdale. Mr. Van Arsdale, Miss O'Toole."

The nurse raised a never-plucked eyebrow. "Pleased," she said, and though by Holly's count she had downed enough Irish to put a strong man under the table, she seemed as sober as when she'd walked through the door three hours before.

"There aren't too many customers left," Clint said. "If you can manage without Holly I'd like to take her home."

"How much have you had to drink?"

"Two beers and three cups of coffee."

"Then I guess it's all right," Pat said begrudgingly. He kissed Holly good-night, and with that same steely look said, "It's late and Holly needs her sleep. Don't be drivin' all over town before you get her home."

"I won't, sir." Clint offered his hand and Pat shook it.

When they were in his car, he said, "Your father wasn't too crazy about my taking you home. Does he carry a shillelagh?"

It was meant to be funny, but Holly didn't laugh. "Why did you come to the Dirty Shame tonight?" she asked.

"I wanted to see you."

Holly leaned her head back against the leather seat. "To talk about the trust fund?"

"No." He pulled up into the driveway of her aunt's house. "To talk about you. Us." He shifted in his seat. "I'm usually a very careful man," he said, "in business as well as in my relationships. I think things through before I act and I never let my emotions get the best of me. My wife left me because she said I was cold and unloving and she was right, I was." He turned toward Holly. "You should know that about me because I'm so damned attracted to you I can't think about anything else."

"Oh." It was an inadequate answer, if indeed it was an answer. Perhaps Clint was, as his wife had said, cold and unloving, but this morning she had seen another side of him. He had held her as gently as he would a child and rocked her fears away. He had kissed her with a fine and fiery passion.

But when he'd left her his eyes had been cold, his voice without expression. He had said, "Alan will always stand between us."

Tonight in her father's saloon he had sat quietly, taking no part in the conviviality around him. He held himself apart; he had spoken to no one.

Alan had been the opposite, filled with life, full of fun, always and forever the life of the party. If he had been at the bar instead of Clint tonight he would have joked with the men and danced with their wives. He'd have joined them around the piano. And he would have drunk more than two beers and three cups of coffee.

Clint got out of the car and came around to help her out. He took her arm when they started up her front steps. When he held out his hand she gave him her key. He opened the door. "May I come in for a moment?" he asked, and when Holly nodded they went inside together.

"Would you like a cup of coffee?"

He shook his head. "It's been a long day for you, I'm sure you're tired."

"Yes, I am."

"About what I said just now..." He hesitated. "I wanted you to understand, to know what kind of a man I am. You're Alan's widow. If we... If I allowed myself to get involved with you I'd feel as though I was betraying him."

Holly turned away from him. "I understand," she said stiffly.

"No, you don't." Clint put his hand flat against the door and shut it. He took a step toward her and, taking her by her shoulders, said, "Don't you think I'd like it to happen between us? Don't you know how much I want you?"

"Let me go."

He stared down at her, and in his gray eyes there was an expression she had never seen before. "No," he said. "I won't let you go." He put his arms around her and kissed her with all of the emotion, all of the passion, he had tried so hard to keep locked up inside him.

"I want you," he said against her lips. "I want to make love to you, with you."

"No!" she whispered against his lips. "Let me go, Clint. I don't want—"

He kissed her again, kissed her until his body hardened with a fierce and raging need and he knew he wanted her as he had never wanted a woman before.

He ravaged her mouth and rained kisses over her face. His body shook with need and when her arms encircled his neck and her body leaned into his he knew he could no longer hold back.

He fumbled with the buttons of her blouse, heard them pop and hit the floor. He cupped the fullness of her breast and when he ran his thumb across her nipple she cried out, "No, don't! Oh, don't!"

But when he took her cry, when he pressed her closer, she swayed against him, her body heated, her mouth as hungry as his.

There was a terrible need in him now, a fire that caught and flamed, and he knew if he didn't have her he would go mad.

With a cry he picked her up and started for the stairs. She said, "No, no, we shouldn't. We mustn't." But when he covered her mouth with his she answered his kiss and clung to him.

At the top of the stairs, he said, "Which is your room?" and when she pointed to it, he carried her in and laid her on the bed.

"Do you remember that day in the grove?" He leaned over her. "The day you fell into my arms."

"I remember." In a voice so low he could barely hear. "I remember."

"I wanted to make love to you then, to forget you were only seventeen and that you were Alan's girl. I wanted to lie with you there, to love with you there."

"I knew," she whispered.

He unbuttoned his shirt and pulled it up out of his pants. He unbuckled his belt; he opened his pants and, after he had kicked his shoes off, he shoved his pants down over his hips. Clad only in his briefs, he began to undress her.

She looked up at him and in the light of the bedside lamp her eyes were sea green, frightened, yet excited. He slipped the white blouse off her shoulders and unfastened her bra. Her breasts were high and full, the nipples small and pink, peaked as though waiting for his touch, his mouth.

He kneeled over her on the bed, straddling her. He cupped her breasts. She watched him, her eyes wide. He squeezed both nipples and when she moaned he leaned to kiss her mouth.

"Holly," he said against her lips. And if a part of his mind cautioned that this was madness, then so be it. He didn't care.

"I've wanted this," he whispered against her lips. "Lord, how I've wanted this." He rose up over her. "But I won't, I won't do this if you don't want . . ." He stopped, all but grinding his teeth against the need that tightened his body. "If you don't want—"

"I want," she said.

A breath shuddered through him. His expression changed, softened.

"My sweet Holly." He kissed her breasts. He licked the satin-smooth skin and circled a nipple with his tongue before he took it between his teeth to lap and to suckle.

Her body arched. She said, "Oh, Clint. Clint." And the sound of her voice calling his name, the way he'd dreamed someday she would call to him, almost sent him over the edge.

He pulled off her sandals, then her skirt. He caught his breath when he saw the black lace panties, and hesitated before he reached to pull them down over her hips. When he had he lifted her higher up onto the bed. He took his briefs off and came into the bed beside her, over her. He fastened his hands in her hair as though afraid she would escape. He took her mouth; he pressed his naked body to hers and the feel of her, all silk and satin softness against his hard maleness, was a joy unlike anything he had ever known.

"I can't wait," he whispered, and gripping her hips he joined his body to hers.

For a moment she felt as though she would faint. The force of him, his strength, his overpowering masculinity, was almost too much for her. He took her mouth and kissed her with all the fever that was in his blood. He plunged against her, plunged and withdrew until her senses reeled, until she lifted her body to his and held him as he held her, with her arms and with her legs. She sought his mouth and pressed her lips to his, her tongue to his. He left her mouth for her breast. He sucked at her nipple. He took the peak between his teeth to bite and tease and when he did she cried out, "Oh, please! Please!"

"Tell me..." he panted. "Tell me if this is good for you."

"Oh, Clint... Clint." Her body rose to meet his and she spun out of control, lost in the magic of a feeling unlike any other, crying his name, whimpering with a pleasure so keen it was both an agony and an ecstasy.

"Say my name again," he cried. "Know that this is me. Say my name!"

"Clint..." A smothered scream. "Clint!"

His body arched, went deep into her and arched again. He cried out and shook as though he had been touched by an electric charge. He rained kisses over her face, her throat, her breasts. He lay over her, holding her so tightly she could scarcely breathe. He said her name again and again. "Holly. Holly." He leaned his head upon her breast and held her close.

In a little while he moved to lay on his side. "I was too rough, too fast," he murmured. "I didn't mean to be. I'm sorry."

She reached up to stroke his hair back from his forehead. "You weren't too rough," she said.

"It was too fast."

She smiled. "If it hadn't been I might not have survived."

He smiled, too, and felt the tension ease, knowing it had been good for her and that she felt as he did. He put his arms around her and she rested her head against his shoulder. The curtains moved with a breeze that came in off the Gulf, cooling their heated bodies, bringing the scent of honeysuckle and night-blooming jasmine into the room.

He felt more at peace than he'd ever felt before and, closing his eyes, thought, I'll rest for a little while. Only a little while. And went to sleep, holding her close.

Holly listened to his even breathing and knew that he slept. But she did not. She disentangled herself enough to reach up and snap off the bedside light. Clint mumbled, "Don't leave me," and tightened his arms around her.

She wasn't sorry for having made love with him, but she knew in her heart it hadn't been a wise thing to do. There had been one Van Arsdale in her life; she didn't need another. Jonah had all but disowned Alan when he married her. What would he do if he knew that she and Clint were ... She wondered what the expression was. Having an affair? Seeing each other? Making love? *Did* love have anything to do with it or was it, for him, a desire that had to be fulfilled, a temporary passion that once satisfied he would need no more?

So many troubling thoughts. So many. And at last she, too, slept.

He came slowly awake. For a moment he was disoriented. The room was dark and unfamiliar. He wasn't in his own bed. Little by little he became aware of Holly beside him, snugged into his arms, her head on his shoulder, one arm around his waist. Instantly then, as if a bugle had blown calling all the troops to attention, he grew hard as a rock.

Strange. He could go for months without a woman, keeping his mind busy with other things—the management of the groves, his work in the senate, a dozen and one matters that needed his attention.

He'd scoffed at weaker men who seemed obsessed with sex and let it rule their lives. But for the past week it had been all he could think about. Somewhere in the back of his mind had been the thought that if he could have Holly once he would be satisfied. He knew now that wasn't so. They'd made love only a couple of hours ago and he wanted her again, wanted her with an urgency that made his back teeth ache.

He tilted her chin up and kissed her gently. She murmured against his lips, but didn't awaken. He turned her toward him and with his arms encircling her back began to kiss her breasts.

She sighed, said, "Umm," and with a lazy cat stretch put her arms around his neck. "Thought you were asleep," she murmured.

"I woke up."

She felt his hardness against her thigh, chuckled and said, "So I see."

He wasn't accustomed to this easy banter. It was something he'd never indulged in while making love, even with Beth. He wasn't a selfish lover. He had always tried to please the women he'd been with, but as with his business or political dealings, making love had always been something to be dealt with, taken care of and wrapped up with the least amount of conversation possible.

He didn't feel like that with Holly. He wanted to take his time with her, tease her, arouse her, touch her and kiss her in a hundred different ways.

He cradled her face between his hands. "It was too fast before," he said. "I want to go slowly this time. I want it to last."

Her last thought before she'd gone to sleep was that they might be embarrassed by this in the morning. Well, it wasn't morning and they weren't embarrassed.

Clint was different than she'd thought he would be, especially now. He kissed her with great tenderness. He stroked her breasts as though afraid he might bruise them. He caressed her shoulders, her back and her belly. He told her how pretty she was and how she made him feel.

He rolled her onto her side and, resting his head against her arm, he kissed her breasts until she thought she would go mad with pleasure. When she said, "So nice, so nice," he eased his hand between her legs and began to stroke her there.

"Will you touch me?" he asked, and when she did he leaned his head against her breasts, moaning softly while he let her minister to him.

He had dreamed of this, dreamed of how it would be if ever they lay together like this. Over the years he'd had as many women as he'd wanted, pretty and willing and inventive young women. But there had been times, in the middle of making love with them, that he'd thought about Holly. He would remember how she had looked up on the ladder in her shorts and the halter that barely covered her ripe young breasts and know that it was her he wanted to be with.

Now she was here in his arms, touching him as he touched her. If this was a dream he never wanted to awaken.

At last he came up over her. He kissed her and, with his mouth on hers, he entered her.

She cried out when he did and he said, "Am I hurting you? Am I—?"

She stopped his words with a kiss. "No," she whispered. "It's just so...so good. You fill me. You make me feel so much."

He kissed her again and, against her lips, he said, "And do you know how you make me feel? When your warmth closes around me, when you hold me inside you?"

He moved against her, slowly, then not so slowly, rejoicing when she lifted her body to his, when she kissed his throat and licked his shoulder and he knew he pleased her. He loved being with her like this, feeling her warmth, pressing his lips to her sweet mouth.

When it began to happen for her, where her breath came fast and her body tightened, when he felt his own swift rise to passion, he said, "Tell me, Holly. Tell me you like this, tell me you want this as much as I do."

But she was beyond words, once again out of control. She could only cling to him, and seek his kiss and call his name in a wonderful frenzy of ecstasy.

"Yes!" he cried, and thrust hard against her, into her and with her in this spectacular moment of glory.

They clung to each other, hearts beating hard. He kissed her; he held her. And wondered how he would ever let her go.

Clint awoke to the smell of bacon frying and coffee perking. He stretched, then sat up and looked around the room. Holly's room. It looked as neat and fresh as she always did.

There was a small easy chair near the window, a dressing table, a dresser, pictures on the wall. A Monet print, a small painting of a seascape, another of an Indian woman with a child strapped to her back. Her mother's and father's wedding picture.

Photographs on the dresser. He got up and went to look at them. There was one of a young woman who looked like Holly, one of a younger Pat grinning into the camera. A picture of Holly in her cap and gown. An eight-by-ten of Alan in a silver frame.

He picked it up. His brother, tall and handsome, standing on the deck of their sailboat with the wind ruffling his hair back from his forehead, wearing trunks, smiling into the camera. It had been taken the summer he turned twenty, just before he and Holly eloped. Scrawled across the picture were the words, "To Holly, my best girl. Now, tomorrow and always."

Always. With an unsteady hand Clint put the photograph back on the dresser. He stood, hands clenched to his sides, his expression tortured, eyes closed against the pain. Pain because he had made love with Alan's wife. Alan was dead and he had made love with his wife. My God.

He went into the bathroom, into the shower. He scrubbed at his skin as though to wash away the memory of how it had been. And when he dressed he went down to the kitchen.

Sun poured in through the curtains and the screened-in back door. The two cats sunned themselves on the stoop outside. Holly, wearing a short skirt and an off-the-shoulder white blouse, was at the stove. She looked as beautiful and as fresh as springtime.

"Good morning." She turned the bacon and, holding the fork, went to him and kissed the side of his face. "Did you sleep well?"

"Yes, fine."

"Hungry?"

"I don't usually eat in the morning."

"But you should," she said with mock severity. "It's the most important meal of the day."

"Who says?"

"My father."

Her father. He had a mental picture of Pat Moran striding through the door, shotgun in hand. "Listen," he said. "I'd better get going."

"But you haven't had breakfast."

"I told you, I never eat breakfast."

"Is something wrong?"

"No, of course not." But he wouldn't look at her.

She turned the fire off under the bacon.

He wanted to go to her, wanted to put his arms around her and hold her close. But he couldn't because making love with her had been a mistake.

"I'll call you," he said, and headed for the door.

She didn't say anything.

He went to her then. He put his hands on her shoulders and said, "Last night meant a lot to me, Holly. I want you to know that."

"But," she said. And waited.

"It wasn't a good idea."

"I see."

"I hope you understand."

She felt cold, so cold. She raised her face and, looking into his eyes, said, "Goodbye, Clint."

He hesitated, then without a word he let her go.

When the door closed behind him she went to the rocking chair beside the fireplace. She sat down, closed her eyes and began to rock back and forth. It was quiet in the kitchen now. She could smell the bacon she would not eat, the coffee she would not drink.

She thought about how it had been last night, how in passion she had cried his name.

She didn't cry. What she felt went too deep for tears. She only sat there in the sunny kitchen, rocking, rocking.

Chapter Six

"Where in the hell have you been?" Jonah looked up from a plate filled with ham and eggs, grits afloat with melted butter and pancakes swimming in maple syrup. "Damn near time you got home."

"I wasn't aware I had to report my comings and goings." Clint poured himself a cup of coffee and pulled out a chair at the end of the table.

"Out catting around by the look of you."

He didn't bother answering.

"Who with?"

Ignoring the question, Clint said, "I had a call from Sanchez in Wauchula yesterday. He's going to have to hire more migrant workers. I told him to go ahead."

"Uh-huh." Jonah sopped up half a runny egg with a piece of biscuit. "So who is she? I hope to God it isn't the Moran woman."

"And what would you do if it was?"

"I'd run her shanty Irish butt right out of town." Jonah shot him a look, then wiped a dribble of egg off his chin. "If you think for one damned minute I'm gonna sit still and let that happen you got one hell of a think coming. Swear to God, Clint, if I thought that you slept with your brother's wife—"

"His widow," Clint said.

Jonah's face went still, his body stiffened. "God almighty," he said. "You have."

"Whether I have or I haven't isn't your affair."

"But she's no good! She ruined your brother's life and now she's after you."

"That's enough!"

"Not anywhere near half enough!" Jonah roared. "She killed your brother and now she's come back for his money. What kind of a man are you?"

"My own man. Remember that. I respect you because you're my father, but I don't take orders from you or anybody else." Clint stood and faced Jonah. "As for the money, Holly was Alan's wife. I think she's entitled to a portion of the trust."

"She's entitled to bird droppings and, by God, as long as I'm alive that's what she'll get. You call Paul Samuels and tell him so. Tell him to look over the papers of the fund and make damn sure there aren't any loopholes."

Clint shook his head. "I won't do that. You said you'd fixed it so there aren't. That ought to satisfy you."

"Well, it don't."

Clint shoved his chair back from the table. "I'm going to change and then drive on over to Wauchula and talk to Sanchez. I'll be back tonight and we can talk about this again if you want to." At the door he stopped and, looking back at his father, said, "But you're wrong about Holly. She isn't the kind of woman you think she is."

When Clint went out and closed the door behind him, Jonah sat for a moment, his face thoughtful. Finally he heaved himself up out of his chair and, as fast as his more than three-hundred-pound weight would permit, hurried to the phone. He dialed and when someone answered, he said, "Give me McCord. Tell him it's Jonah Van Arsdale."

While he waited Jonah drummed sausage-fat fingers on the breakfront. When McCord came on the phone he said, "I want to see you right away." He listened, then barked, "I don't give a damn what you've got to do, this is important." He looked at his watch. "Eleven's fine. I'll be waiting."

Jonah's face relaxed when he put the phone down. McCord was the best private investigator in the business. He'd worked for Jonah before. McCord knew his business; he'd get enough on the Moran woman to send her running back to New Orleans on the first bus out of town. If she didn't go of her own free will he'd personally see to it that she did a little time at the county work farm. One way or the other, he'd make damn sure she never set foot in Braxton Beach again. She'd ruined one of his sons; he wasn't going to stand by while she ruined another.

Nurse O'Toole was coming out of Aunt Lou's room when Holly got to the hospital that morning. Before Holly could enter, the nurse said, "Just a moment," and motioned her toward the nurses' station.

"What is it?" Holly asked, alarmed.

"Your aunt's had a setback. She won't be going home today."

"What happened?"

"She's got an abscess and she's developed an infection. The doctor's treating her with a different antibiotic. We've got to keep an eye on her. I called your father a few minutes ago to let him know. He's coming over soon as he gets a chance."

Holly gripped the edge of the counter. Taking a deep breath to steady herself, she asked, "How serious is it?"

"Serious enough to keep her here for a while. Infections like this can take time. The doctor will explain everything to you and your father when he comes. Now go along and see your aunt. She's upset because she can't go home. Try to assure her that she's all right, but that we need to keep her here awhile longer."

"I will."

"And don't look so worried." O'Toole started to turn away, then hesitated and asked, "Anything wrong? Besides worrying about your aunt I mean?"

"No." Holly shook her head. "Not really."

"Your dad told me you were married to the younger Van Arsdale son. Didn't know him. Guess the two of you were gone by the time I came to Braxton Beach. His brother's sure a good-looking man. Got a build like a gladiator and a look in his eye that'd scare the hell out of the lions and send a woman running for cover or right straight into his arms."

"Unless the woman knew she'd be better off taking her chances with the lions."

Miss O'Toole's eyebrows rose. "So that's how it is," she said. And with something that might have been a smile hurried on down the hall.

Holly spent the day in her aunt's room. When her father arrived he said, "You look worse than Lou."

Holly forced a smile and, glancing over at her sleeping aunt, said, "I'm all right."

"What's going on with you and Clint?"

"Nothing, why?"

"You're not getting mixed up with him, are you?"

"Of course not."

"Then how come he hung around the Dirty Shame till almost two just so he could drive you home?"

"He wanted to talk about Alan's trust fund. If Alan had lived he would have come into a million dollars on his thirtieth birthday. Clint thinks I came back because of it, that I'm going to claim I have a right to it."

"You got any interest in a million dollars?"

"Not *that* million dollars."

"Then tell Clint and his father to put the money where the sun never shines," Aunt Lou said from the bed.

Pat laughed. "That's telling 'em, old girl." He went over to the bed and took her hand. "How are you feeling, darlin'?"

"Like I've gone through the tumble cycle and been hung out to dry. What's the matter with me?"

"You've got a little infection," Holly said, "and you're on a different antibiotic. Don't worry, you're going to be fine."

"I don't feel fine. How're the cats?"

"Fat and lazy."

"That's good. I think I'll sleep awhile now."

Pat kissed her cheek and, when Lou dozed again, he said, "You look done in, Holly. Best you go home and get a good night's rest."

"I will in a little while," she assured him. When he left she sat in a chair beside the bed. Her aunt's color was bad and her breathing labored. When the doctor came in he checked Lou's chart and examined her hip. When he was through he motioned Holly out of the room.

"We're hoping the new antibiotic will help," he said, looking worried. "But patients react differently. If she hasn't improved by tomorrow we'll try something else."

And if that doesn't work? Holly wondered, but was too afraid to ask. When she went back into the room Aunt Lou wanted to know what the doctor'd said.

"That you'll feel better as soon as the new antibiotic takes hold."

"Maybe yes, maybe no. I want you to see Alex Harwood. He's the one who made up my will. Go talk to him tomorrow and make sure everything's in order."

"You can talk to him yourself as soon as you're out of the hospital."

"No," Lou said. "I want you to do it. I want to make sure everything is all right. Promise me you'll go see him tomorrow."

And finally Holly said she would.

She stayed by her aunt's bedside all that day and she was still there when the Reverend Richardson came that evening. He chatted with her aunt for a little while and when he left he insisted that Holly have dinner with him.

They went to the same restaurant on the wharf she'd gone to with Clint. It wasn't until they were seated that she saw Clint seated at a table adjacent to the one they were led to. He was with two other men. He looked from her to the minister and his face tightened.

"Good evening," Reverend Richardson said. "Nice to see you, Mr. Van Arsdale."

"Good evening." He nodded to the minister, then said, "Holly."

She tried to concentrate on what Edward Richardson was saying, but it was difficult because she was so conscious of Clint at the next table.

They had missed her at choir practice, the minister said. He understood, of course, that between visiting her aunt in the hospital and helping her father out she had very little time for anything else.

He told her about growing up in Maine and said he'd come to Florida because he'd had enough of the freezing winters. "And because of the fishing," he said. "The first thing I did when I got here was to buy a boat. She isn't much to look at, but she's seaworthy. I hope you'll come out with me sometime."

"I won't be in Braxton Beach very long. As soon as Aunt Lou's better I'll go back to New Orleans. I have a job and a home there."

"Why don't you just stay in Braxton Beach?"

"There's nothing for me here."

"Your father and your aunt are here." His nice brown eyes softened. "And so am I, Holly."

She didn't know how to respond. She searched for something to say, but before she could, Clint and the men he was with rose to leave and Clint came to their table.

"I thought your aunt was coming home today," he said to Holly.

"She's had a setback. We're not sure now when she'll get out of the hospital."

Clint looked from Holly to the minister. He said, "Don't let me disturb your dinner," and with a nod turned away.

"Strange," Richardson said. "Mr. Van Arsdale seemed upset about something. He's your brother-in-law, isn't he? How do you get along with him?"

"All right, I guess." But as she said the words the memory of last night crept like an unwanted shadow into Holly's mind. She heard again the muted whispers and sighs, the frantic sound of "Oh, please, oh, please, oh, please..."

"Holly?"

She clamped down on her bottom lip and, coming back to the reality of the now, said, "I didn't have any contact with either Clint or his father after I left Braxton Beach."

"They weren't in touch with you when your husband was killed?"

Holly shook her head. "Mr. Van Arsdale came to Marathon to claim Alan's body and bring him back here for burial. Clint was in Morocco when it happened and he flew directly to Braxton Beach."

"You weren't able to return for the funeral?"

"No, I was still in the hospital."

"How long have you been away?"

"Almost eight years."

"Have you..." Edward cleared his throat. "Have you had any thoughts of marrying again?"

"No," she said quickly. "No."

The waiter brought their dinner. The minister waited until he'd left, then said, "My wife died almost five years ago."

"I'm sorry. I didn't know."

"We'd known each other since we were children so she'd been a part of my life for almost all of my life."

"That must have been hard."

"Yes, it was. But moving to Florida helped and so did my new ministry. Time eventually heals almost all of our wounds, Holly, and finally there comes a time to move on with our lives." His eyes were warm, his expression gentle. "With other people," he said.

"That isn't always easy." She busied herself buttering a piece of roll. "Tell me about your boat. What kind is it?"

She knew that he didn't want to change the subject, but he did, gracefully. He talked about his boat, about fishing, and as soon as they finished he signaled for the check. When they arrived at her aunt's house he walked her to the door. "Good night," he said. "Rest well."

"Good night, Edward. Thank you for dinner."

He took her hands in his. "I know how worried you are about your aunt. If there's anything I can do, if you need to talk to anyone, please call me."

"I will. Thank you."

"Well, then . . ." He reached out to her, then stopped and, turning away, hurried down the steps.

When she went in the two cats yowled a greeting. She toed out of her shoes and headed for the kitchen where she opened a can of cat food and fed the cats. As soon as that was done she went upstairs, ran a hot bath and filled the tub with scented oil.

She put a Patsy Cline tape on and, when the tub was full, lowered herself into the hot water, closed her eyes and let the music surround her. For this little time she wouldn't think; she'd just lie here and let her bones melt.

For a while that's what she did, but thoughts kept drifting through her brain. Of Edward Richardson. A kind and gentle man. A man she would never be interested in.

And though she tried not to, she thought about Clint. Last night she had lain in his arms. She had lifted her body to his and cried his name. Yet tonight he had looked at her as though she were a stranger.

"Crazy..." Patsy sang.

She wasn't sure how last night had happened. It shouldn't have. She hadn't wanted anybody, hadn't been with anybody since Alan. But she'd gone to bed with his brother.

"Crazy for lovin'..."

Lovin'. No! She mustn't even think the word. It had been a mistake. Clint knew it. He was sorry it had happened and so was she.

Don't think about it. Don't think about anything. Let the warm water soothe the body tired from a long day at the hospital, tired from last night's...

"Lovin'," Patsy sang.

Holly got out of the tub and, when she was dry, wrapped herself in a terry-cloth robe and brushed her hair. She had just started down the stairs when the front doorbell rang.

"Who in the world?" she muttered, and headed for the door. But when she started to open it she remembered what had happened with Buford and said, "Who's there?"

"Clint."

Clint? She hesitated, then opened the door a few inches. "What is it?" she asked.

"May I come in?"

"I was almost ready for bed." But she opened the door.

He looked around. "Are you alone?"

"Of course I'm alone," she said indignantly, sorry now that she'd let him in.

"What's going on with you and the minister?"

"Nothing."

"It sure as hell looked like something."

"He went to the hospital to see Aunt Lou. Before he left he asked me to have dinner with him."

"Does he look at everybody in his congregation the way he was looking at you tonight?"

"He was just being nice."

"Sure. Look, could we sit down for a minute? I won't stay long."

It wasn't a good idea, but she found herself saying, "All right, let's go in the kitchen. I'm going to make some cocoa. Would you like a cup or would you rather have coffee?"

"Do you have anything stronger?"

"Aunt Lou has a bottle of sherry."

"I'll pass. Just coffee if it isn't too much trouble."

"It'll be instant."

"That's fine."

He followed her out and took a stool at the bar while she fixed coffee for him, cocoa for herself and filled a plate with chocolate-chip cookies. She must have just come from her bath, he thought. Her skin looked rosy and when she moved closer he caught the scent of summer roses. She was barefoot; her toenails were pink.

She put both cups in the microwave and, when the hot drinks were ready, said, "What did you want to see me about?"

It took him a minute to tear his gaze from her pink toenails and answer, "A couple of things."

He hadn't meant to come here tonight, but something had happened to him when he'd seen Holly with the minister. He'd never been jealous before, not with Beth, not with any of the women he'd known, but it had taken every bit of his willpower not to go for Richardson's throat.

"About last night," he said.

Holly looked at him, teeth clamped on her bottom lip, eyes gone suddenly too big for her face.

"It was..." He looked down at his coffee, then raised his gaze to hers. "It was heaven on earth," he said softly. "You made me feel so much, Holly. So incredibly much." He reached for her hand. "But I think we both know it shouldn't have happened."

Holly didn't say anything; she only looked at him.

"I'm sorry..." He took a deep breath. "No," he said. "That's a lie, I'll never be sorry that we were together that way."

"I think I understand how you feel," she said. "There are too many memories between us. Alan was your brother, I was his wife. We can't change the way it was."

"No, we can't." He stroked the back of her hand. "I'm sorry," he said again.

"Yes, so am I."

He let go of her hand. "I know you don't want to, but we have to talk about the trust fund."

"Clint, I—"

"I'll speak to our lawyer," he said, stopping her. "I'm sure something can be worked out."

Holly stirred her cocoa, stirred and stirred while she tried to frame an answer. At last she said, "Maybe I didn't make it clear before. I didn't come to Braxton Beach because of Alan's trust fund, I came because of Aunt Lou."

"But you knew about the money."

"Yes. I told you that Alan discussed it with me. But that was almost eight years ago. A lot has happened since then." She took a sip of her cocoa. It was hot and sweet and comforting. "I could have used money after the accident," she said, "but at the time I was too hurt, too devastated by Alan's death, to think about money or anything else.''

She had been hurt. It was strange, but in all these years he'd thought of the accident only in terms of his brother, never about what might have happened to Holly. He put the cup down. "How badly were you hurt?" he asked.

"My leg was broken, my shoulder and three ribs. The sternum was cracked and there were..." She paused. "Internal injuries. I was in the hospital for almost a month.''

She'd been what? Twenty-one? Twenty-two? Injured, in pain, her young husband dead. My God.

"I didn't know," he said. "I was only thinking about Alan. I'm so sorry, Holly.''

Sorry. She looked away from him and all the old bitterness came back, the memory of those pain-filled days in the hospital. And afterward, when she'd felt so alone but determined to pull her life together. She had been too proud to take money from her father and as soon as she could, before she'd really recovered, she'd gotten a job waiting tables at a restaurant in Marathon. It had been hard. There had been nights when she'd lain awake, crying with fatigue and pain, longing for Alan, haunted by the memory of his death.

Now, her voice tight with emotion, she said, "I could have used some of Alan's money to help pay my hospital bills, Clint. For the car that had been totaled but not paid for, for so many unpaid bills.''

"Bills that you'd run up, Holly.''

She looked at him, surprised.

"Alan wrote me about how extravagant you were. There was hardly a month passed that he didn't write me for money." Clint frowned down at his coffee, and when he lifted it to drink it left a bitter taste in his mouth. "Alan was doing the best he could," he went on. "I know you were young, Holly, and I don't blame you, but the poor kid was breaking his back trying to keep you happy."

"I . . . I didn't know he asked you for money."

"He didn't want to go to Dad." Clint looked at her and with a shake of his head said, "There's so much I need to know about those years. How you and Alan lived, about his work, so many things. You said the past was past, but it isn't for me because I want to know about Alan and about you. He was my younger brother, Holly. I loved him."

"So did I," she said.

She closed her eyes and for the first time he saw the dark patches of fatigue under her eyes, the lines of strain around her mouth. She looked very young, very fragile. Her robe had fallen open, exposing one leg, and it occurred to him that because she'd just come from her bath she probably didn't have anything on under the robe. And though he had told both himself and Holly that what happened last night must never happen again, he felt an urgent and overwhelming need to take her in his arms and carry her up the stairs to her room.

But because he didn't want to feel that way, because it was easier for him to think of her as his brother's wife, his brother's widow, he said, "Let's get back to the trust fund."

"Oh, yes. The money." A sad smile curved her lips. "I'd forgotten that's why you came."

"I think we can work out a reasonable compromise. Dad will raise hell but I don't need his okay in making a decision." He got up, shoved his hands in his pockets and, after he had paced back and forth a couple of times, said, "How does a quarter of a million sound?"

Holly shook her head as though puzzled. "A quarter of a million? I don't want a quarter of a million."

"I won't agree to a penny more than that. Take it or leave it."

"I leave it."

"What?"

"I don't want your money, Clint," she said, getting angry. "I don't want anything from your father or from you. You can take your money and..." She stopped, remembering what Aunt Lou had said today in the hospital, bit back the words and said, "I'm very tired. I think you'd better go."

"Listen," he said. "I—" He stopped. She had leaned her head on her hand as though suddenly too tired to hold her head up. The dark cloud of her hair partially hid her face. He said, "Holly?" and when she didn't answer he rested his hand on the top of her head and said, "Go to bed. We can talk about this tomorrow."

She raised her face. The anger had vanished and he saw only sadness. "I wish you would believe me," she said. "I wish I could tell you..."

He lifted her down from the stool. She stiffened, but when she tried to step away he tightened his hands. "Who are you?" he said. "What do you want?"

"Just to be left alone," she whispered.

He almost believed her. God knows he wanted to. He held her away so that he could look at her, look deep into eyes that were as green as the far-out deep waters of the Gulf. He wanted to lie with her tonight, to hold and comfort her, and because he knew that he should not, he brought her into his arms and held her there. With all his heart he longed to wipe the past away and pretend there was only the here and now and that they could begin again as though they had only just met, as though there had never been Alan.

But Alan had been real. He had lived and he had died, and neither Clint nor Holly could ever forget that.

Clint let her go and stepped back. "It's late," he said, because he knew if he stayed a moment longer, if she kept looking at him with her eyes gone slumberous and soft, he wouldn't be able to leave.

"I have to go." His voice was rough with all he was feeling. And when she didn't move, he said, "Go to bed, Holly. Just . . . go to bed."

He turned away and hurried from the kitchen. At the front door he stopped and looked back. She stood framed in the doorway between the kitchen and the living room, silhouetted in the glow of lamplight.

It took every bit of his willpower to turn and walk away.

Chapter Seven

As tired as she was, Holly slept very little that night. What disturbed her the most was the ambivalence of her feelings about Clint. She had told herself before she returned that she wanted nothing to do with the Van Arsdales and that she would do her best to avoid them. Yet less than two weeks later she had gone to bed with Clint. She needed to have her head examined.

It shamed and embarrassed her that Alan, without her knowledge, had borrowed money from Clint and that Clint thought she was responsible for their financial troubles. No wonder he was convinced she'd come back to Braxton Beach for money!

Unable to sleep, she thought back to the early years of her marriage to Alan. For the first six months she had been so in love that none of the realities of life touched her. She loved the small apartment they rented two blocks from the ocean in south beach. The Murphy bed was lumpy, the springs in the two overstuffed chairs were broken and the toilet leaked. But it didn't matter. They were young and they were in love.

Those first few months, partly because they had so little money and partly because she didn't know how to cook, they lived on scrambled eggs and peanut butter sandwiches. When their money ran out Alan got a job tending bar. After a week or two he told the owner about Holly and she'd been hired to sing on weekends.

It was the first time she'd ever sung professionally and she was scared to death. But the customers liked her and both she and Alan got tips. They still ate scrambled eggs and peanut butter sandwiches, but with their tips were able to eat out once or twice a week, either in one of the Jewish delicatessens she loved or a Cuban place he liked.

Those were the happiest six months of her marriage. But things changed when Alan went to work for Island Rum International as an assistant in their public-relations office. The company was owned by the father of one of Alan's drinking buddies from Florida State. Junior Garcia's father had come from Cuba as a young man. His father had owned a big rum distillery there, and as soon as Junior's father could, he went into business in Miami. By the late seventies he ran the largest distillery in the southeast.

Part of Alan's job involved romancing clients, wining and dining the big wholesalers who bought their product, arranging cocktail parties and receptions, fishing trips for out-of-town buyers and, during racing season, taking them to the track. He became a familiar figure at Hialeah and Gulfstream when the horses ran, at the dog track when the horse-racing season ended.

It was the perfect job for Alan. He was young, good-looking and affable. Clients liked him and so did their wives. He drank with them; he gambled with them. He opened charge accounts and spent more money than he had on clothes.

"It's part of the job," he told Holly when she worried about his spending money they didn't have. "I have to look good, it's part of what I do."

They moved to a bigger apartment and when she said, "We don't need all this space," he told her that entertaining at home was part of his job.

He made good money, but it disappeared too quickly. By the end of every month they were usually broke.

Alan started drinking too much. He went to the track, not just with out-of-town buyers, but on his own, alone. He gambled heavily. When he won he'd splurge—buy her a new dress, take her to dinner at the Fontainbleau or the Doral, fly over to Nassau to play the gaming tables. When he lost, when the money was gone, she took a job as a waitress.

He didn't want her to. "How would it look if my boss came in and saw you waiting tables?" he said. "It's bad enough you're singing in that sleazy joint on weekends, but waiting tables?"

"We're two months behind in the rent," she said. "We need the money."

He made a killing at Hialeah and traded the car his father had given him when he'd started at Florida State for a newer, sportier model. That was the car that had been totaled in the accident that killed him.

He drank to celebrate when he won, to lessen his dismay when he lost. He got drunk at a company party one night and got into a fight with a customer who did a million-dollar business with Island Rum every year. Garcia gave him the word, shape up or ship out. He stopped drinking. For a while.

Every year Island Rum entertained a hundred of their best customers at an island bash. That year the island was Puerto Rico and Alan was put in charge of the arrangements. He bought a new gown for Holly, an expensive suit for himself.

There was a gambling casino in the hotel, a big, beautiful room with chandeliers and pretty young ladies who passed out the free rum drinks. Alan lost heavily. The more he lost the more he drank.

On the night of the farewell banquet, which he had arranged and was supposed to oversee, Holly had to drag him away from the gaming tables. He wasn't exactly sober, but he could have pulled it off if he hadn't had any more to drink. But he did. And it cost him his job.

He went back to work as a bartender. When he was fired from there he got a job selling shoes at Burdines. He cut down on his drinking and he stopped gambling. He went to see Mr. Garcia and when he agreed to go into an alcohol abuse program Mr. Garcia took him back.

Things improved. The last three months of their marriage had been relatively happy. Even that last weekend down in the Keys had been happy, at least at the beginning.

So many memories. Good memories of the time when she had first been in love; bad memories of falling out of love. For the past few years she'd been able to put the past aside and go on with her life. But now, because of Clint, everything had come back to her.

At seven that morning, tired from her almost sleepless night, Holly rose, took her shower and, when she was dressed, called the hospital. The nurse on duty told her that her aunt had had a restless night but that her condition was stable. Stable. A word that could mean just about anything.

Holly waited until nine-thirty before she called Alex Harwood's office. He said he could see her at ten. When she got to his office, in the same building as every other attorney in Braxton Beach, she took the elevator to the fourth floor and was ushered into his office by his secretary.

Harwood rose and came around the desk to give her a hug. "Heard your aunt was ailing," he said. "When's she coming out of the hospital?"

"We're not sure. She's on a stronger antibiotic and we're hoping that will take care of the problem. She wanted me to talk to you about her will, to make sure everything was in order."

He looked immediately concerned. "Is she that serious?" he asked.

"I don't think so, but she insisted I see you and I didn't want to upset her."

"Well, sure." Harwood went to one of the file cabinets and when he found her aunt's file returned to his desk. "It's a simple document," he said when he opened it. "She's leaving the house and furnishings to you, along with the money in her bank account." He grinned. "With the stipulation that you take care of her cats."

"That's it?"

"Yep. You tell her everything's in order and that all she has to do now is get well."

"I will." Holly stood to shake hands and said, "Thanks for seeing me, Mr. Harwood."

"No trouble, Holly. You give your aunt my best. I'll stop by and see her as soon as she's home."

She was smiling when she left the office and stepped into the elevator. Just as the doors closed, she heard someone running down the hall call out, "Hold it!" She put her hand out, the doors jiggled but didn't close and Clint hurried in.

He looked at her, surprised, looked at the office she'd just come from and saw the words Alexander T. Harwood, Attorney at Law, on the office door.

His expression changed. "I see you didn't waste any time seeing a lawyer," he said. "You know, it's funny. I actually believed you last night when you said you didn't want anything."

His anger took her by surprise. She said, "No... no, you don't understand. I went to see Mr. Harwood because of Aunt Lou. She wanted me to—"

"Come on," Clint said, his mouth twisting in disgust. "Stop trying to kid me. You thought it over after I left and decided the quarter of a million wasn't enough. Decided maybe you'd go after all of it. Or is it more than that, Holly? Maybe you're after Alan's share of everything."

The elevator doors opened and they stepped out. Before she could protest, he took her arm and led her farther down the hall away from anybody coming in or going out of the building.

"All right," he said. "Tell me the truth."

"Clint, please..."

"I wanted to believe you." His eyes were tortured. "My God, Holly, you don't know how badly I wanted to believe you when you said you weren't interested in the money."

"You don't understand," she said. "Clint, please, listen to me. I..." But he'd already turned and walked away.

She stood there, frozen, sick with shame and anger. She wanted to go back to her aunt's, pack her bag and head out of town. But she couldn't. Aunt Lou needed her; she had to stay. Clint could think whatever he wanted to. It didn't matter.

Then why did she feel so empty, so bereft? Why did she feel as if a door had been slammed in her face?

She went into the ladies' room where she splashed cold water on her face and told herself that nothing he said mattered. That he didn't matter. But that didn't change the emptiness inside her. Or the pain.

In the days that followed, Clint worked from morning until midnight. He drove from grove to grove, from Braxton Beach to Wauchula, on over to Sebring, to Homosassa, to Yankeetown and Dunnellon. He raised hell with the men he'd put in charge of the groves, and at night in whatever motel he was in he drank himself into a stupor because he thought the liquor would help him sleep.

He did everything, anything, he could not to think about Holly. But in the darkness of the night, in a lonely bed in some one-horse town, he lay awake remembering another night. And with fists clenched called himself a fool because he couldn't get her out of his mind. Finally, when he knew that running away wouldn't help, he returned to Braxton Beach.

"Got something to show you," Jonah said that first night at dinner.

"What?" Clint looked up from the food he had barely touched.

"You remember McCord?"

"The P.I.? Yes, I remember him. Why?"

"Had him doing a little work for me."

"What about?"

"The Moran woman."

Clint turned on his father, frowning. "You had him investigating Holly? Why in the hell did you do that?"

"You know damn well why!" Jonah stabbed his fork into a piece of blood-rare steak. "I've been right about her all along. You'll see when you read it. I put in on the desk in your office."

Clint didn't like it. He told himself he wouldn't read it, but after dinner he took a glass and a bottle of brandy and went to his office. The report was in a brown envelope on his desk. He poured himself half a glass of brandy and opened the envelope.

The first few pages detailed the three years she and Alan had lived in Miami Beach. There was a photograph of the outside of the first apartment they'd lived in. Beside it McCord had written, "They paid three hundred a month rent for a studio here."

Next was a notation of the neighborhood bar where Alan had worked as a bartender and Holly had sung on weekends. That was followed by a glowing report of the year and a half Alan worked for Island Rum International.

"Although Mr. Van Arsdale made a handsome salary with Island Rum and they moved to a fifteen-hundred-dollar-a-month apartment, after only a few months his wife got a job as a singer in south beach at night."

McCord went on to list the various bars and clubs she'd sung in, noting the category of the place after each name—Fredo's South Beach, sleazy; The Mousetrap, a pickup joint; The Five O'Clock Club, not too bad.

And later, after Alan's death, other places, in Key West, Marathon, Plantation. The club in New Orleans.

"High-class and expensive," McCord noted. "Owned by Jacques Dupre. Checked him out. He's forty-five, good-looking and rich. I don't have proof, but from what I've heard from some of the people I talked to in the French Quarter I'd say that Dupre is keeping her. She owns a pretty nice house in the Garden District and drives a late-model car. The odds are good that everything doesn't come from the salary she makes singing at the Parisiene."

Clint drank the half glass of brandy and didn't even feel it go down. The name Jacques Dupre burned in his brain. Jacques Dupre. Jacques Dupre.

"The accident." McCord had underlined the two words in red. It had happened near Fiesta Key, at dusk on a late Monday afternoon. It had been raining. According to the police report the road was slick. Mrs. Van Arsdale had been driving. She smashed into a bridge abutment. No other car was involved. She and Mr. Van Arsdale were taken to the hospital in Marathon. Mr. Van Arsdale died before they reached the hospital. There had been a half-opened bottle of Scotch on the front seat of the car.

Clint wasn't aware he'd finished the brandy until he picked up the bottle to refill his glass and realized it was empty. He rubbed a hand across his face and continued to read.

"Mrs. Van Arsdale, five months' pregnant at the time of the accident..." The words swam before his eyes. He stared at the report. Read it again. "Five months' pregnant at the time of the accident, miscarried the baby."

He went as hollow inside as though he'd been kicked. He closed his eyes and it seemed to him that he could see her there on the rain-swept highway, her husband fatally injured, herself hurt, bleeding, knowing she was losing her baby. Dear God.

He picked up his glass, then put it down again. There was so much he didn't know about her, so much he needed to know. About Jacques Dupre. About her real reason for coming to Braxton Beach.

She'd told him she hadn't gone to Harwood's office about the trust fund, but he hadn't believed her. What if he'd been wrong? He'd already jumped to too many conclusions about her.

He reached in the desk drawer for the phone book. Harwood, A., Attorney at Law. An office number, a home number. He dialed the home number.

A woman answered. He asked to speak to Harwood. She said, "Just a minute."

When Harwood came on the line, Clint said, "This is Clint Van Arsdale, Mr. Harwood."

"Hey," Harwood said. "How're you?"

"Fine, thank you. I'm sorry to be calling you at home, but there's something I need to know." He hesitated. "It's about Miss Moran. Holly."

"What about her?"

"I saw her coming out of your office last week. It's fairly urgent that I know why she came to see you."

"Privileged info, Clint."

"I know that." He gripped the phone. "I don't want details, but if it's about the money—"

"What money?"

Clint swore under his breath and tried for patience. "From the trust fund," he said.

"Don't know what you're talking about."

"Alan would have come into quite a bit of money from a trust fund on his thirtieth birthday. I believe that Holly feels she's entitled to it. I agree that she should have a portion of it and I—"

"You're barking up the wrong tree, son. I don't know a damn thing about any trust fund."

"But I saw her coming out of your office."

"Maybe you did, but why she was here didn't have a damn thing to do with money excepting for what her Aunt Lou has in the bank." Harwood paused. "Well, hell, I guess it won't do no harm to tell you. Holly came to see me because Lou wanted her to make sure her will was in order."

"Her will?"

"And if you think I'm gonna tell you what's in it you're wrong."

"No, no, I . . ." He couldn't find the words to go on.

"Anything else?" the lawyer asked.

"No. No, and thank you, Mr. Harwood."

Clint put the phone down and stared at the almost-empty bottle. Had to see Holly. Tell her he was sorry. He pushed his chair back and stood. Staggered. He'd be stupid to drive. Didn't matter. Had to see her. Tell her he'd been wrong. Had to.

She was in the kitchen when she heard a car pull into the driveway. It was almost midnight. She felt a clutch of fear. Maybe something had happened to Aunt Lou. She'd seemed better the past few days, but the doctors were still concerned because she was running a low-grade fever. Had she taken a turn for the worse? What if her father, instead of phoning, had come to tell her that Aunt Lou had . . . ?

With a low cry, Holly ran into the living room and flung the door open. "Dad?" she called out. "Is that you?"

"It's me." Clint steadied himself on a porch pillar. "Got to see you." She saw a taxi back out of the driveway.

She stared at him. "You've been drinking."

"Yep. Been drinking. Doesn't matter. Gotta see you. Gotta come in." He shoved past her into the living room, saw the sofa and headed for it.

"You're not welcome here," she said. "I want you to leave."

"In a minute. I'd like a cup of coffee if it's not too much trouble."

Holly stared down at him. "All right," she said. "But you wait here."

"Absolutely. Won't move. Sit right here." He looked up at her. "Like your robe. Meant to tell you when you wore it before. Shouldn't ever wear anything but that robe."

Holly shook her head in exasperation and with a frown headed for the kitchen. "Damn!" she muttered as she fixed a mug of coffee and put it into the microwave. She'd give him coffee, try to sober him up and call a cab, pour him into it and send him home.

When she came back with his mug of strong coffee, he said, "Thank you." Then carefully, formally, "'Fraid I have a small buzz on."

"So it appears."

"'Pologize."

"Just drink your coffee."

He drank half of it, then leaned his head back against the sofa. "Hate a sloppy drunk," he said.

"So do I."

He stayed like that for several minutes. Then he drank the rest of the coffee and asked for another cup. When she came back with it he was asleep. He'd loosened his tie. His dark hair was rumpled; a lock of it fell over his forehead.

She stood over him, not quite sure what she should do. He couldn't leave, not like this. Maybe if she woke him up, gave him more coffee and something to eat... No, she decided, it would be better to let him sleep it off.

She eased him down on the sofa, picked up his legs, brought them up and took his shoes off.

She turned all the lights off except for a small table lamp, then went back to the kitchen and turned the light off there. Back in the living room, she went to the sofa and looked down at him. He was sleeping, but he wasn't peaceful. He was scowling. There was a line of wrinkle on his forehead and patches of fatigue under his eyes.

She felt a sudden and overwhelming urge to smooth the lock of hair back from his forehead. But she didn't. She had no idea why he was here. She could only hope and pray that when he awoke he would leave. Leave her in peace.

With a sigh she turned and went up the stairs to her room.

Chapter Eight

Holly had no idea why Clint had showed up at her door. Or why she had let him in. She should have sent him packing. Why had he wanted to see her? After what he'd said outside Alex Harwood's office last week she knew exactly what he thought of her. Then why was he here?

Frustrated and angry, Holly went to bed. She didn't plan to go to sleep, not with Clint downstairs. She'd just rest for a little while, hopefully long enough for him to sober up, then she'd go downstairs and ask him to leave.

Her eyes drifted closed. She snapped them open. Had to stay awake. Clint was downstairs. What if he...? But for all her trepidation there was a sense of security in knowing somebody else was in the house. Maybe she'd sleep for a little while... just a little... She curled onto her side and, though she didn't mean to, slept the best sleep she had in a week.

And awoke in the first pink light of dawn to find Clint sitting on the edge of her bed. He was naked from the waist up and his hair was wet.

He said, "I took a shower. I hope that's all right."

Holly stared up at him, still in that drowsy half sleeping, half waking stage, trying to get her thoughts together, wondering what he was doing in her bedroom.

"I used your toothbrush."

She brushed the tangle of hair back from her face and remembered.

"I'm sorry about last night," he said. "For coming here when I was drunk."

"Why... why did you?"

"I wanted to apologize for the way I acted outside of Harwood's office. I was out of line, Holly. And wrong. I had to tell you. It couldn't wait till morning."

"I see." She pushed herself up to a sitting position. "What changed your mind?"

"I talked to Harwood."

"Oh."

"I don't deserve your forgiveness, but I'm asking for it."

She became aware then that the sheet had fallen down around her hips and that the thin strap of her nightgown had slipped off one shoulder. She pulled it up, then the sheet.

That brought the suggestion of a smile and he said, "I wonder if you know how you look right now." He twisted a curl of her hair around his finger as his smile faded. "I've been such a bastard, Holly. I've accused you of being after Alan's money and didn't believe you when you told me the truth." He touched the side of her face. "Forgive me. For coming here drunk last night, for being a fool. But most of all forgive me for judging you when I had no right to judge.''

She covered his hand with hers, telling him with that gesture that she forgave him.

''There are so many things I don't understand about you and Alan, but it doesn't matter. I don't care what you've done or where you've been, or Jacques Dupre or anything else.''

''Jacques? But—''

''None of it matters.'' He brushed her hair back from her face. ''I wish I'd known you when you were a little girl. What kind of a child were you? Did you miss your mother the way I missed mine? Were you happy? Were you sad? What books did you read? What kind of games did you play? Dress up?''

He had a sudden, funny and endearing image of her parading around this room in her mother's dress, wobbling on high heels, bright spots of rouge on her cheeks, dime-store beads around her neck, pretending to be all grown up.

He thought of his own growing-up years and knew how painful those years could sometimes be, with what uncertainties a child is possessed, what dreams a child dreamed. Holly had lost her mother, as he had lost his. How that must have frightened her, how hurt she must have been.

''Who was the first boy who kissed you?'' he asked.

Holly smiled. ''Sammy Simoski,'' she said. ''When I was six.''

He put his arms around her and drew her closer. For a little while they stayed like that, leaning back against her pillows. It was enough to hold and be held. And to know that in a little while he would be loving her. Loving Holly. He had never felt this closeness, this sense of peace, with anyone before.

He stroked her hair. He slipped the strap of her gown down and kissed her shoulder. He wondered what it would be like to awaken like this every morning, to see her face, to feel her so warm and soft beside him.

He eased her farther down in the bed so that he could feel the whole length of her beside him. Sweet scents, smooth satin of her gown. He kissed her lips, they parted under his. He cradled her in his arms, holding her tenderly, lovingly. He slipped both straps of her gown down and began to stroke her breasts. She moved closer, filling his hands.

"This is where you belong," he whispered against her lips. "Like this, with me. Making love with me."

And though he liked the feel of the satin against his skin, he needed to feel her naked beside him.

"Raise your arms," he said. When she did he eased the gown up over her head. Then pulled his jeans down over his hips and tossed them away. He brought her back into his arms and the feel of her nakedness made him groan with pleasure. He brought her up over him so that he could feel all of her warmth, the firm mounds of her breasts, her belly, her hips, her marvelous legs. He held her like that, breathing in the aroma of her hair, feeling it splay across his throat, his chest. And knew that this was where she belonged, here with him, like this.

He rained kisses over her face, her throat, her shoulders. He slipped his hands around her waist. He buried his face against her breasts. And said, "Holly, oh, Holly, love."

She felt the rough stubble of unshaven beard against the tender skin of her breasts and clutched his shoulders to hold him there while he suckled and teased. After a few minutes like that, he rolled so that they lay facing each other. He kept kissing her, her mouth, her throat, the lobes of her ears, her breasts.

Her body grew heated and moist and he touched her there, stroked her there. Without his asking her, she began to caress him. His body quivered as though he'd been touched by a live wire and he moved closer, filling her hand, murmuring her name, fighting for control.

He sucked at her lips and kissed the corners of her mouth. He kissed her breasts and took a nipple between his teeth and lapped and nibbled until she cried out as though in pain.

Caught in a whirlwind of feeling and of need, she whispered, "Clint. Clint, please…I…I want you. Now, oh, oh, please."

He came up over her. He grasped her hips and, with a cry that seemed to come from the very center of his being, he joined his body to hers.

Caught in an immensity of feeling that was almost too much to bear, Holly lifted herself to him. She held him with her arms and with her legs. She said his name over and over again like an ancient prayer uttered in an indecipherable tongue.

His cadence quickened. He thrust hard; he withdrew to thrust again. And all the while he showered her with kisses, her face, her throat, her shoulders. He eased his hands under her bottom to raise her closer, and held her there while his big body moved so wildly against hers.

She clung to him, breathless with desire, every nerve alive, burning, heated. This was past bearing, but she didn't want it to stop because now she was a part of him, one with him. Loving it. Loving the body that moved so deeply inside her, the scent and the taste of his skin, the touch of his hands, the feel of his mouth covering hers. Loving . . .

She lifted her body to his and bit back the words she longed to say, words of tenderness, words of love. Oh, love. He kissed her, his tongue hot and sweet when it met hers, and the intimacy of his touch, the tenderness of it, tumbled her over the edge of joy and she spiraled up and up, out of control, crying his name, "Clint! Oh, Clint!" in a paroxysm of ecstasy.

He took her cry, his body shaking with the same wild passion that held her in its grip. They kissed long and deep, kissed and moved against each other until they lay with heart beating against heart, locked in their lovers' embrace.

When at last he made as though to move away, she said, "Not yet. Stay like this. Let me feel you like this." And held him there inside her.

A morning breeze came in through the white curtains to cool their bodies and they lay for a long time without speaking. He stroked her back and kissed the side of her face while they drifted in the lovely afterglow of love.

When he began to grow again they moved ever so slightly against each other in somnolent leisure. Deep, so deep it seemed he touched her very soul. The rise to passion came slowly. He kissed her eyelids, her nose and her mouth. He caressed her breasts and whispered his pleasure against her lips. And when he heard the catch of breath in her throat, when he felt her begin to tremble against him, he whispered, "Tell me, Holly. Tell me, when it happens."

And she said, "Oh, yes. Oh, darling, yes."

Yes. He took her mouth; he took her cry. And tried to tell her with his kiss and with his body what he could not put into words.

Together, holding each other close, they crested the tide of their passion. And when once again she said, "Oh, darling. My darling Clint," he thought his heart would burst with all that he felt for her.

They sat together at the kitchen table, a pot of hot coffee on the stove, bacon and eggs and hot biscuits in front of them. They had showered together, and afterward, though she'd wanted to dress, he had insisted she wear just the robe.

"It's getting to be a fixation," he said with a grin. "A fetish. I've got a thing for your robe."

They smiled at each other across the table. He kept touching her, her hair, her face, the leg exposed when the robe fell open. He wanted to fill his eyes with her, to engrave the picture of her as she looked now into his memory. Yellow robe open at mid-thigh, damp hair curled around her face, mouth soft and swollen from his kisses. Green eyes looking at him with an expression he'd never seen before.

He was beginning to learn her body, learning where to touch her, where to kiss her, to have her moan into his mouth and ask for more. He knew when the soft cries, the whimpers and the pleadings would come. And rejoiced because there was still so much more to learn.

And because he felt that way he wanted to know what was in her heart and her mind. He wanted to fill in the spaces of the years when he had lived in Morocco and she had lived in Miami with Alan. And later, alone, in New Orleans.

He waited until they finished breakfast and were on their third cup of coffee before he said, "Holly, dear, will you tell me about your marriage? About you and Alan?"

She paused, the cup halfway to her mouth. "What . . . what do you want to know?"

"How it was with the two of you. If you were happy." He reached for her hand. "Please," he said. "Tell me."

She withdrew her hand and moved her chair a little away from him, as if to physically remove herself from what she was about to say. "We went to Miami," she said. "We found a studio apartment near the ocean."

He remembered the picture in McCord's report of a rundown building with a dying palm in the front yard.

"It wasn't a very nice place. The furniture was covered with some kind of a purple cabbage design in a chintzy material. Every time we pulled the Murphy bed down I was afraid it would spring up again and lock us against the wall. But it was the only bed we had and . . ." She stopped. Color rose in her cheeks and she lowered her gaze from his.

Their bed. Hers and Alan's bed. He tried not to flinch and said, with what he hoped was a touch of humor, "Not exactly the perfect honeymoon cottage."

The hint of a smile touched her lips. "It was like playing house. I was eighteen and Alan was twenty. We were children pretending to be grown up. We spent our days at the beach. You should have seen him, Clint. His skin turned bronze and his hair was bleached from the sun and salt water. Girls used to turn and look at us." She smiled. "Well, not at us. At him."

"What about money?" Clint asked. "What did you do about money?"

"Alan got a job as a bartender in a little bar not too far from the apartment. He made barely enough for us to skimp by, and when the owner mentioned that he might get somebody to sing weekends Alan suggested me."

"When did Alan get the job with the rum company?"

"About six months later. He wrote to a college friend whose father owned Island Rum. Mr. Garcia hired Alan and he went to work in their public-relations department."

"Alan would have been good at that." Clint stood and went to the stove, got the coffeepot and refilled both their cups. "I imagine he made pretty good money there."

"Yes." Holly warmed her hands around the cup. "Yes, he made very good money. We moved to a nicer, expensive apartment and . . . and I decided to go back to work."

"Why? Didn't Alan make enough to keep you happy?"

"It wasn't that." She looked down at her coffee. "I guess we spent a lot of money on . . . on things."

She'd been young, he told himself. It was only natural she'd want nice things, clothes, jewelry. But Alan had been young, too, working, trying to do his best to keep her happy. How difficult it must have been for him.

Under the table he clenched his hands together and said, "Tell me about the weekend he was killed, Holly. It happened down in the Keys?"

Holly nodded. "It was a company thing, a party at Mr. Garcia's home in Key West. All of the company executives were there with their wives. On Saturday most of the men went deep-sea fishing and on Saturday night there was a party."

"With a lot of drinking."

Holly looked down at her hands. "Yes."

"Were you and Alan drinking?"

"No, I . . . I don't drink."

Don't or didn't? he wondered, but did not ask. "What about Sunday?" he said.

"Some of the men went fishing again, some of them played golf."

"What about Alan?"

"He ... we stayed at the house with a few other people."

"And drank."

She wanted to stop, but she was held, trapped by the intensity of Clint's eyes. "Alan ... Alan had a few drinks."

"But not you." Clint pushed the half-empty cup of cold coffee away. "What about Monday?"

"It rained. We left in the afternoon."

"And you were driving?"

Holly looked at him, then away. "Yes," she said. "I was driving."

"What happened? The police report said there wasn't any other car involved in the accident."

"I ... I don't remember. I must have skidded off the road."

Her face was bone white. He wanted to stop, but something pushed him on. He looked away from her, balled his hands into fists and asked, "He wasn't killed instantly?"

"No. They—the highway patrolmen—when they finally came they laid him on the ground next to me. It was raining and his face was wet. It took a long time for the ambulance to come."

Oh, God, such a long time. They took her out of the car first and laid her on the wet grass at the side of the road. She held her hands over her stomach as though that way she could keep her baby safe. But she knew, knew the life inside of her was dying.

She called out to Alan and a woman from one of the cars that had stopped knelt beside her and said, "It's going to be all right, it's going to be all right." But the woman was crying, too.

She reached for Alan's hand. It was cold and wet. His face was white, his body looked broken. They put her on the stretcher and she screamed because some of the shock had worn off and pain cut like a bright hot poker through her body. Somebody took her hand and put a needle into a vein in her arm. She said, "My baby! My baby!" and a man in a white jacket said, "Oh, God, she's pregnant," and somebody else said, "She's hemorrhaging."

"Holly?" Clint said, "Holly?" and she looked at him as if for a moment she didn't see him.

"It was a long ride back to Marathon," she said. "They had the siren on. It sounded like screaming. I wanted to hold Alan's hand, but they had tubes in my arms and they wouldn't let me. I kept saying, 'Alan? Alan, please answer me,' but he didn't."

She looked down at her cup and drank cold coffee without knowing it was cold.

He hated himself for making her do this. But he had to know how it had been.

"Someone called my father and your father," she said.

"Yes, I know. Dad hired a private plane and flew to Marathon." Without asking her father to go along even though he knew Pat Moran would want to be with Holly. How could Jonah have done that? Hadn't he known that Pat Moran was suffering the same terrible fear, the anxiety, that he felt? Their children had been hurt. How heartless of Jonah not to have asked Holly's father to come with him.

Clint stood and went over to the fireplace. He told himself that what had happened had been an accident, a terrible accident. But the thought that it could have been prevented gnawed at him. If it hadn't been raining, if Holly hadn't been driving... The report said there'd been an open bottle on the front seat. Which one of them had been drinking?

Had she told him everything or had she held back? Were there things she didn't want him to know?

There was a side of him that wanted to leave it alone, to leave the questions unanswered. Holly had been through enough, he didn't want her to suffer any more than she already had. But Alan was his brother. Was blood thicker than water or was love the most important thing of all?

Love. He turned then and saw her still at the table, silent, unmoving. Her cloud-dark hair only partially hid her face. He could see the strain there, the agony that remembering had brought.

In two strides he crossed the room and, lifting her out of her chair, brought her into his arms. He felt her stiffen, but he held her there, warming and comforting her. He whispered soothing words and kissed the top of her head. "I'm sorry," he said. "Sorry I made you go through that. I won't again, Holly. I swear I won't."

A sigh quivered through her. "Clint," she said. "Clint, there's something I have to tell you. Something I should have told you before. About the accident. I wasn't—"

The phone rang, shrill and sharp, cutting her off.

"What, Holly? What?"

"Wait till I answer the phone," she said.

She crossed the room and picked it up. She said, "Hello? What? Oh, my God!" Then, "Yes, of course.

I'll be there in a few minutes. No, no, don't call my father. I will."

She put the phone down. "What is it?" Clint asked. "What's happened?"

"My aunt. She's worse. She has pneumonia. I've got to call my father."

"You get dressed. I'll call your dad."

Her eyes were frightened. For a moment she stood as though unable to move, then she said, "All right. Yes, call him."

He called her father and told him he'd go to the hospital with Holly. He cleared the table and put the dishes in the sink. When Holly was ready they hurried out to her car. "There are new drugs," he said. "Your aunt will be all right."

Holly didn't answer. When they got to the hospital he parked. Before he could come around to open her door she was out and running toward the entrance. He ran after her and together they went up to her aunt's room. Her father was already there. Her aunt was in an oxygen tent.

Pat Moran put his arms around Holly. "It's serious, lass," he said. When he let her go he shook Clint's hand. "Thanks for coming with her, Mr. Van Arsdale." If he wondered what Clint had been doing at Holly's at nine in the morning or why he hadn't shaved, he didn't ask.

Nurse O'Toole came in. She rested her hand on Pat's shoulder, gave it a squeeze and to Holly said, "Your aunt's a strong lady, she'll pull out of this." She nodded in Clint's direction. "Her doctor has called in a specialist. He saw her earlier and he'll be back in a little while to talk to you."

Holly moved a chair over to her aunt's bedside. She took her hand and said, "Aunt Lou? Daddy and I are here, Aunt Lou."

Lou's eyelids fluttered. She looked up and when she tried to speak the nurse lifted the plastic tent.

"Such a fuss," Lou whispered.

"You need to rest," O'Toole said.

"But I've got company," she said, and her eyes drifted closed.

The new doctor came in. He listened to Lou's chest, consulted her chart, then motioned the three of them outside.

"We won't know anything for a few hours," he told them. "I've ordered a stronger antibiotic and I'm hoping it'll do the trick. I was going to order a special nurse for tonight, but Miss O'Toole has offered to stay with her." He grinned. "I've dealt with O'Toole before so I know better than to argue once she's made up her mind."

When the doctor left they went back into the room. Clint, because he felt out of place and thought father and daughter might want to be alone, excused himself. He said he'd be back later and that Holly or her father should call if they needed anything. He shook hands with Pat, then put his arms around Holly and kissed her.

"What's goin' on between the two of you?" Pat asked when Clint left.

"I'm not sure."

"You're fallin' for him, aren't you?" And before she could answer he said, "Lord, Holly! You've had one Van Arsdale in your life, you don't need another."

They didn't talk much after that. Nurse O'Toole went off duty with the promise that she'd be back later. Other nurses came and went. They gave Aunt Lou shots; they changed the IV. In the late afternoon Pat had to leave to open the saloon, but Holly stayed.

Clint returned that evening. He said, "Let me take you to dinner."

Holly shook her head just as Rosie O'Toole sailed into the room, all stiff and starch efficiency. She checked Aunt Lou, then asked Holly if she'd had anything to eat.

"I'm trying to get her to go out for dinner," Clint said.

"Try harder," O'Toole snapped. She turned to Holly. "You go ahead to dinner. Afterward, if you want, you can come back and check on Miss Lou. But I'm going to be here all night. I've promised your father, and I'll promise you, that if there's any change I'll call. I know you're worried. So'm I, but I got a hunch this aunt of yours is going to make it. She's going to be all right and so are you if you'll stop looking so scared and go along with tall, dark and good-looking." She nodded to Clint. "Where you taking her?"

"The Chop House. And here's my car phone number."

"Fine. If I need to I'll call you."

"Tough lady," he said when he and Holly were alone.

"I've got a feeling my dad's crazy about her."

He whistled. "Brave man if he is."

He tried to keep the conversation light on the way to the restaurant and all through dinner. When they finished he drove Holly back to the hospital and went in with her. O'Toole said everything was under control. She said there was only one good chair in the room and she intended sitting in it so Holly might as well go home.

Holly argued. The nurse remained firm. She was here, and here she would stay till morning. Holly could come

back then, as early as she wanted, but it was best she
went home now.

Clint agreed. There wasn't any point in Holly spending the night at the hospital.

She argued with him on the way out to his car and all
the way back to Aunt Lou's house. He didn't even
bother to answer. When they got to the house he told
her, without asking if he could, that he was going to stay
the night.

"You don't have to do that," she said.

"I want to." He smiled. "I even brought my own
toothbrush."

They went in. After she fed the two cats he took her
hand and they went upstairs to her room. She was suddenly tired, too emotionally exhausted to protest when
he eased her down on the bed and began to undress her.

"I should take a shower," she said.

"We both will."

It seemed natural that they would shower together. He
wanted to bathe her and, content to let him, she leaned
against the shower wall while he soaped her body. His
hands were strong and smooth and infinitely comforting.

When they came out of the shower he toweled her dry
and, taking her hand, led her to bed and came in beside
her. But he made no attempt to make love to her. He
only held her, patting her as though she were a child,
rubbing her back, gently kissing the side of her face.

And at last she slept, cradled in the warmth of his
arms.

It was only later, on the edge of sleep, that he remembered she had started to tell him something earlier today. He wondered what it was, just before he, too, went
to sleep.

Chapter Nine

The new antibiotic worked. Aunt Lou rallied and the oxygen tent was removed. But the pneumonia had weakened her; it would take a while to regain her strength.

Clint sent fresh flowers every day, and every night he came by the hospital to take Holly to dinner and home to spend the night with her.

And once, knowing that she was treading in deep water as far as her emotions were concerned, she said, "What about your father, Clint? What does he think about your being away from home every night?"

"I'm my own man," he said. "I have been since I went away to Tulane. I live my own life. I don't report to my father. For five or six months of the year we share the same house and I oversee the groves. The rest of the time I'm in Tallahassee. I've had a house there for the

past three years, ever since I've been in the state senate.
I consider it my home."

"He's never forgiven me for marrying Alan, has he?"

Clint hesitated. He wanted to lie, to tell her that his
father had softened over the years. But Jonah hadn't
softened. He'd never forgiven Alan; he would never
forgive Holly. The very mention of her name infuriated
him. As far as he was concerned she was still that saloon girl from the wrong side of town who'd run off with
his younger son and had been responsible for his death.

His father was a difficult man, and though Clint respected him because he was his father, he wasn't blind to
Jonah's faults. He'd known for a long time now how
powerful his father was, for though Jonah himself was
not politically active, he was the power behind half of
the elected as well as the appointed officials in this part
of Florida.

When Jonah had suggested—no, not suggested—
when he insisted Clint run for the Florida state senate,
Clint had told him he had no interest in politics. Then
he'd thought it over and decided that, after all, he would
make a run for it because he honestly believed he could
make a difference. During his three years in the senate
he had never once allowed his father's opinions to influence any of his own political opinions, his decisions,
of what was right and good for Florida. He knew in his
heart that he was a good senator, that he had done his
very best to do what was right for the people in this part
of Florida.

He and his father disagreed on many things. Holly
was one of them. Jonah's opinion, his prejudice about
Holly, would not influence Clint. He knew what kind of
a woman she was; he knew how much he was coming to
care for her.

The nights they spent together were as close to heaven as he ever hoped to get. Never before had he shared this kind of intimacy with anyone, an intimacy that went far beyond the sexual pleasure he experienced with her. He loved sitting at the kitchen table with her in the evening, drinking coffee with her while the two cats watched them with sleepy yellow eyes.

Whatever tensions he had experienced during the day were forgotten in the warmth of the kitchen. He told her about what he'd done that day, about driving over to Sebring to check on the groves there or to Orlando to consult with his constituents. He asked her about her aunt; he worried with her and laughed with her when she talked about her father's growing attraction for Rosie O'Toole.

He eagerly looked forward to that time of evening when they would go upstairs together. Sometimes they showered together, sometimes they soaked in the big, claw-footed bathtub together. He would bathe her and tease her, and as the days passed he came to know her body, to know from the sudden slumberous expression in her eyes, the softening of her mouth and the whisper of a half-smothered gasp, exactly how aroused she was becoming. With soapy hands he would caress her breasts, sublimating his own rise of passion because he loved exciting her like this, knowing that soon, when he joined his body to hers, she would welcome him with her warmth, her glad cry of passion.

She was everything he had ever dreamed a woman could be; he loved every moment he spent with her. And yet . . . and yet there were times just after they had made love when the thought of Alan would force its way into his consciousness. Holly had been Alan's wife. She had lain with him, as she now lay with Clint. With the thought of how it had been with his brother and Holly, he would be overcome with guilt. She had been Alan's wife, how could she be like this with Alan's brother?

One morning, alone in her room after she had gone downstairs, he took Alan's picture off the dresser and put it in a drawer. If she was aware that it was gone, she never mentioned it.

She had started going to choir practice again, and on the Sunday before Miss Lou left the hospital, he went to church with Holly.

He sat in the back as he had that other Sunday and watched as, with the minister leading the way, the choir started down the aisle in a two-by-two formation. They wore white robes with royal blue satin collars, six men and six women singing, "All Hail the Power." When Holly passed him, her head bent over the hymnal, she looked up and smiled. A smile for him.

He barely listened as the service began, nor did he join in the singing of the hymns. When she rose to sing a solo, "Blest Be the Morn," he felt a tightness in his chest, and closed his eyes to let the sound of her clear, sweet voice wash over him.

"Blest be the morn," she sang, "for this new and blessed day."

This blessed day, this time with Holly. It was then, listening with his eyes closed, that he knew he loved her. But he did not know what he was going to do about it.

"I've seen him watching you," Aunt Lou said on the morning before she was to leave the hospital. "I know there's something going on with you and Clint, but I'm not sure what it is. I reckon he's out-of-his-mind crazy about you, though."

Holly shot her aunt a grin. "Is he?"

Aunt Lou chuckled. "Listen here, missy. Just because I've never married doesn't mean I don't know when a man's got his eye on a woman. I know he likes you, same's I know your daddy's got the hots for that O'Toole woman."

"Aunt Lou!" Holly laughed. "Shame on you, talking that way."

"Facts are facts. Your daddy's been bit by the love bug and so has Clint Van Arsdale." She leaned her head back against the pillows and motioned Holly to sit beside her. "I like what I've seen of Clint, but the idea of you being mixed up with another Van Arsdale scares me to death."

"It scares me, too."

"He brought you to the hospital the morning I took bad. It was early, he hadn't shaved, and in my book that means he probably spent the night somewhere beside his own house. My guess is he's been spending a lot of nights with you."

Hot color crept into Holly's cheeks, but before she could say anything, Aunt Lou took her hand and said, "Clint's a fine-looking man and I've got a hunch he's a better man, a stronger man, than his brother was. But he's still a Van Arsdale, Holly, with a daddy who's mean as a cottonmouth. Jonah Van Arsdale pretty much runs this part of Florida and it scares me to death thinking what he might do if he thought Clint had some serious intentions toward you. Jonah's got it in his head that Clint's going to go on to the United States senate just like his own daddy did, and when Clint does Jonah'll be wanting some highfalutin society woman for Clint to marry, not a..." Lou hesitated. "You know what I'm talking about."

"Not a saloon girl," Holly said.

"That's about the size of it. The Van Arsdales belong on their side of town, we belong on the other side."

But do we? Holly wondered. Hadn't the times changed from when, in small towns like Braxton Beach, one section of society lived on one side of the tracks and poorer, blue-collar folks lived on the other side? This wasn't the fifties, it was the nineties. True, her father owned a saloon. But he was a respected member of the community with a multitude of friends. People looked up to him. Did that make him less important than a man like Jonah Van Arsdale? Of course it didn't. Nor did it make her unsuitable for a man like Clint.

She didn't know what was going to happen in their relationship, but she knew that whether it worked or not wouldn't depend on which side of town she was from.

Clint had never expressed his feelings or his intentions. She knew he cared for her, but did caring mean love? And if he loved her would he still let the memory of Alan come between them?

She hadn't noticed until this morning that Alan's picture was no longer on the dresser. A little stunned, she had opened the drawer and seen it, facedown, among her scarves. It had been thoughtless of her not to put it there herself. Of course having Alan's picture in her bedroom would bother Clint. Did he feel guilty? And would he, because she had been his brother's wife, ever be able to put aside his guilt and have a lasting relationship with her?

Her aunt was being released from the hospital the following day, so she and Clint would no longer be able to spend the nights together. Would this be the time for him to back away, to ease out of the relationship?

In another two or three weeks Aunt Lou would have sufficiently recovered and Holly could make plans to return to New Orleans. She had a home there, a job and friends. Perhaps that's where she belonged.

"Holly?" Aunt Lou patted her hand. "You've gone off woolgathering. Thinking about Clint, weren't you?"

"Yes," Holly admitted.

"Maybe instead you should be thinking about the man you wrote me about. Your boss in New Orleans."

"Jacques," Holly said. "He's a very nice man who doesn't believe in marriage."

"*That* kind." Lou shook her head. "Well, there're other fish in the sea besides minnows and sharks."

Minnows and sharks, Holly thought when she left the hospital that night. Jacques and Clint.

Jacques had called her once a week since she'd left New Orleans. The last time he said, "When are you coming back, *ma chérie?* I miss you. The customers miss you. The maître d' at Antoine's misses you."

"My aunt is still in the hospital," Holly told him. "It will be at least two weeks before I can even think about leaving."

"You sound tired."

"I've been spending a lot of time at the hospital."

"How about a week in Hawaii when you return? I know this wonderful hotel in Maui where we could—"

"Jacques!"

"Paris?" he said. "Athens? A cruise around the Greek islands?"

"You're crazy," she said with a laugh.

"About you, *ma petite.* You miss me a little, yes?"

"A little."

"You know I'm mad about you, Holly."

"Just mad," she said. "Just mad."

"Enough to do something I said I'd never do."

"What?" she asked, amused. "Have dinner at a fast-food restaurant? Buy a hot dog off the street? Wear blue jeans instead of a pin-striped suit?"

"Mon Dieu," he said in mock horror. "What do you take me for." His voice sobered. "I'm almost fifty, Holly. Perhaps it's time..." He sounded nervous. "I don't want to do this on the phone, *chérie,* but there is a most important question I will ask you when you return."

Another proposition, Holly wondered when she hung up the phone. Or was it something else? Was Jacques going to ask her to marry him? She hoped not, for though she liked him and they had fun together, she didn't, nor would she ever, think of him in that way. Jacques was fun, but— Suddenly, like it sometimes happened in comic strips, a light bulb went on in her brain and she remembered Clint had mentioned Jacques's name. She hadn't thought of it when it happened because she'd been so emotionally shaken recounting the events of Alan's death. But she remembered now. How in the world did Clint know about Jacques?

That night when they were once again seated at the kitchen table in her aunt's house, she said, "How do you know about Jacques Dupre?"

Clint looked startled, then embarrassed. "You...well, I suppose you mentioned his name."

Holly shook her head. "I don't think I did, Clint. I can't imagine where you heard it."

He didn't want to tell her; he was ashamed to say that his father had hired a P.I. to investigate her. But he had no choice. He reached for her hand. "My father hired a private eye to have you investigated," he said. "I saw the report."

Holly stared at him. "Investigated?"

"He suspected I had been seeing you. I guess he thought if I knew about Dupre I'd back off."

"I see." She withdrew her hand and, getting up, went to the stove. That Jonah had hired someone to check up on her didn't surprise her all that much. The fact that Clint hadn't told her did.

When she had poured more coffee she took a sip of hers, then said, "Jacques Dupre is my boss. I've known him for almost three years. He heard me sing at the Five O'Clock Club in Miami Beach and offered me a job making double what I made there. His offer was too good to turn down."

Clint tightened his hands around his coffee cup. "The offer or the salary?"

Holly raised her chin and looked him square in the eye. Without directly answering his question, she said, "A month after I went to work for Jacques at the Parisiene he asked me to become his mistress. I refused and when I threatened to quit he backed off." She took a sip of coffee. "At least once every six months he brings the subject up again."

His hands were cold. He warmed them around the cup and waited for her to go on.

"I'm fond of Jacques," she said. "He's been a good friend to me. But my answer has always been the same, a firm and definite no." She stirred her coffee. "So in answer to your question, Clint, Jacques and I have never been lovers. We never will be." She paused, wondering whether or not to tell him of her last conversation with Jacques. Then she decided that since she'd already told him so much he might as well know the rest, and said, "He called me a few days ago. I think, from what he said, that when I go back to New Orleans he's going to ask me to marry him."

"But you wouldn't!" He jostled his cup and the coffee spilled over the side. "You're not in love with him."

"No, I'm not."

"Then why do you want to go back to New Orleans?"

"It's where I live. It's my home."

He wanted to tell her not to go. He wanted to say, Stay here with me, Holly. Give us a chance. But something held him back.

"I wish you'd told me about the investigator," she said. "You should have."

"Yes." He reached for her hand again and this time she didn't draw away. "I'm sorry my father did it," he said. "I'm sorry I didn't tell you. Will you forgive me?"

"I forgive you, Clint, but this... this thing with the private eye, his spying into my life in New Orleans, the suspicion..." She lifted her shoulders in a gesture of resignation. "I think it's pretty clear that this... this whatever is between us can't go on. There are too many things that stand between us. Alan, your father."

"No." He stood and, taking her hands, brought her up beside him. "I won't accept that." He kissed her and, though she seemed reluctant to answer his kiss at first, little by little her lips softened under his. And when they did he swept her up in his arms and carried her up the stairs toward her room.

His excitement grew with every step, excitement mixed with the fear that he might lose her.

Once in the bedroom he quickly undressed her, tearing one of the buttons on her blouse in his haste to touch her. He pushed the blouse open, and with a low groan buried his head between her breasts.

"Unfasten my belt," he said, and when she did he unzipped his trousers and squirmed out of them. The desire to make love with her was so intense he felt as though his body was on fire.

Their clothes were scattered on the floor. She said, "Wait," but he was beyond hearing. Too impatient to throw back the bedspread, he laid her down on top of it. There were no thoughts now, only the need to have her.

He came up over her. "I want you," he said. "I need you. Dear Lord, Holly, do you know how much I need you?"

"Clint," she whispered. "Oh, darling..."

The word, that one word, was almost his undoing. With a cry he covered her body with his and, gripping her hips, he took her.

Her breath quickened. She held him, she sought his mouth and touched her tongue to his. He moved against her with a sense of desperation, as though by doing this he could drive all other thought from his mind. And from hers. There was only the now, with Holly holding him, moving with him.

In that final moment when her breath became ragged and she whispered her plea for release, when she said, "Oh, darling, darling, darling," he cried out, a primitive cry that seemed wrenched from somewhere deep inside of him.

"Holly," he said against her lips. "Oh, Holly."

He held her, kissed her and slept holding her close in his arms. To dream... Sweet dreams of Holly and that long-ago summer in the orange grove. Holly up in the tree, the sack of oranges over her shoulder. Cute little bottom cupped by her shorts. As though in slow motion he saw her fall, not quickly as she had, but floating gently downward as he ran forward to catch her.

He felt the airy weight of her in his arms, then they were falling...down, down to the ground with the oranges tumbled around them. He felt the grass beneath them; he smelled the oranges. And her skin. He held her in his arms. She said, "Oh, darling," as she had when they made love and his body yearned to possess her. He eased himself over her...and awoke, rigid and burning with need.

He touched her, he stroked her and when, half-awake, she turned to him, he joined his body to hers. Slowly, easily, he filled her with the essence of himself. She took him in, cradling him to her breasts, and when the moment came she whispered once again the words, "Oh, darling. My darling."

He went to sleep with his body over hers. And the scent of oranges filling the room.

The following day Aunt Lou was allowed to return home. Hattie Hellinger, who'd been her twice-a-week cleaning woman for the past twenty years, came to work full-time. And Nurse O'Toole—"Only because she's trying to make points with your father," Aunt Lou said—volunteered to look in on Lou every day.

But it was Holly who supervised her aunt's care. She talked to Clint on the phone, but several days went by without their getting together.

"I'll arrange something," he said. "A trip out of town. Something."

Troubled by his own demons, he tried to keep busy. When he wasn't overseeing the groves he worked in the office going over the books. And when he wasn't checking the books he met with his constituents. He'd be up for reelection next year; it was time to start lining things up.

"One more turn in the state senate," his father said one afternoon when they were having lunch, "and we'll go for the United States senate. Old Hank Trefren'll be over eighty by then and ready to retire. The minute he says he is, you announce."

Clint wasn't sure that was what he wanted. He wasn't sure about much of anything except his need to be with Holly. Sometimes he went a whole thirty minutes without thinking about her, about how she looked that last morning when they made love, how the sunlight coming in through the windows made patterns of gold against her skin, the way her dark hair brushed his chest, the muted sounds she made just before the final moments when her body lifted to his. He was obsessed with her, consumed by his need for her. But always, somewhere in the back of his mind, was the thought of his brother, that Holly had lived with and had loved his brother.

And, too, there was the thought of what had really happened the weekend Alan had died. There were some things in the P.I.'s report that troubled him. Holly had told him she didn't drink and he believed her. Especially since she'd been pregnant at the time. So if she hadn't been drinking how had the accident happened? And why hadn't she told him about the baby? McCord had checked the police reports, but what if he had missed something? What if he'd only told Jonah what his father wanted to hear? Maybe he should ask McCord to go back to Key West. Maybe he'd go himself, talk to the police there, have a look at the reports.

Finally he decided to call McCord.

The P.I., after the first greeting, didn't seem too anxious to talk to him. When Clint told him he wanted to discuss the investigation of Holly Moran, McCord asked, "What for?"

"There are some things in the report that I think need checking again, a few questions I'd like answered."

"Yeah, well..." He heard the hesitation in Mc-Cord's voice.

"It's important," Clint said. "I'll pay you for your time and for whatever additional information you might have."

"Okay," the P.I. said. "I can meet you tomorrow at the Hitching Post. One-thirty?"

"That's fine." Clint put the phone down, not sure he'd done the right thing. But determined to go through with it.

McCord was waiting for him when he walked into the Hitching Post the following day. The detective, decked out in jeans and boots, a Western shirt and leather vest, with a ten-gallon hat on the chair beside him, went with the decor.

He looked up from a Dos Equis dark when he spotted Clint and motioned him to the chair across from him.

"Want a beer?"

Clint shook his head. "Just coffee."

"Beer goes better with chili. Cools the pipes."

"Okay, a beer."

McCord signaled to the waitress and a frizzy-haired woman with a big rear end hurried over. "Another beer and two bowls of your red-hot chili, sweetheart," he said.

"Goin' to fry your gizzard, McCord. Had you clutching your throat and rolling your eyes last week when you were here."

McCord laughed. "Appreciation, girl. Sheer appreciation." He turned to Clint and when they were alone he leaned back in his chair. "But you didn't come here to talk about chili, did you?"

"No." Clint looked across the table at him. "I told you last night, I want to talk about your investigation of Miss Moran. There were a couple of things that bothered me."

McCord took a long pull of his beer. "Like what?"

"I'm wondering if you put everything you should have in the report."

The P.I. picked up his beer. He finished it and signaled to the waitress that he wanted another one. When she brought it he said, "All right, maybe there were a couple of things I left out of my report to your father."

"Such as?"

"Such as I don't think your brother's widow was driving at the time of the accident."

Clint stared at the other man. "What in the hell are you talking about? The police report said—"

"I know what the police report said, Mr. Van Arsdale. But I was a cop in L.A. for almost twenty years before I decided to pack it in and be my own boss. I saw so many freeway accidents I almost knew before I got to the scene what it was going to be. If it came on the radio they hadn't used seat belts I'd know for sure I was going to be seeing a bloody mess. I knew what kind of injuries the driver'd probably have and what kind of shape the passenger would be in."

He took a long swallow of his beer. "After you called last night I took another look at the pictures that were taken at the time of your brother's accident in the Keys. No other car was involved. It was a Monday afternoon when there wasn't all that much traffic. I wondered about that the first time I checked the photos. I'm still wondering."

"But I read the police reports," Clint said. "They said that my brother wasn't driving."

"The blows he took on his forehead and his nose were made by the steering wheel, not the dashboard." McCord took another pull of his beer. "What I didn't tell your old man was that your brother'd had three previous arrests for drunken driving. His license had been revoked for a year a month before the accident. One more offense and it would have meant six months in the clink. Especially since he was driving without a license."

"But if that's true it seems to me even more evidence that he wasn't driving the day of the accident."

"Maybe yes, maybe no. Let's just suppose he was driving and that he was drunk when they had the accident. His wife would have known that this time it meant jail. What if she decided to take the blame? What if she pulled him over and got behind the wheel before anybody found them?"

"You're guessing," Clint said. For though he wanted to believe McCord, he wasn't sure he did. Maybe McCord was making this up as he went along, telling him what he thought he wanted to hear.

"What I did, Van Arsdale, was give your father the facts off the police report, but there were some things I didn't tell him. There were inconsistencies in the police report so I decided to check out a few things myself."

McCord hitched his chair closer. "I've got friends in Miami, cops I've worked with, a few connections. It was pretty well-known in the area that your brother was a big-time spender. He drank too much and he gambled—on the horses, dogs, football, anything he could. He gambled big and he lost big. He wore expensive clothes and lived in a high-class Miami Beach apartment. The only hitch was that his wife had to go to work to pay for it."

Clint thought about the day he'd asked Holly if Alan didn't make enough money to keep her happy. She hadn't answered him. If what McCord said was true, she'd worked to keep them going.

"I checked the arrest warrants with Miami PD," McCord went on. "And a couple of days ago I talked to Raul Garcia, the president and CEO of Island Rum International. Your brother worked for Garcia for a year and a half. He was one hell of a good PR man, Garcia said, but he was drinking too much, first with clients, then on the job. Garcia fired him because of it.

"A few months before the accident your brother went to see Garcia. He told him he hadn't touched a drop in weeks and pleaded for his old job back. Garcia gave in. He said that for a while Alan was fine, as sharp and as good as when he'd first come with the company."

The waitress came with the chili. She looked at McCord, then at Clint, said, "How 'bout if I keep these warm for you?" and took off.

"There was a big company party at Garcia's home in Key West the weekend of the accident," McCord went on. "He gave a party like that once a year for his executives and their wives. The men and however many of the wives who wanted to spent three days deep-sea fishing, playing golf and living it up.

"Your brother fished on Saturday, hooked into a six-foot marlin and celebrated with a couple of rum-and-colas. By Saturday night he was loaded. When he started drinking on Sunday his wife tried to stop him. He slapped her. Garcia and a couple of the men and their wives saw it."

"Alan wouldn't do that." Clint's lips were as white as his face. "Either you're making it up or they're lying."

"I'll give you their names," McCord said. "You can talk to them if you don't believe me." He picked up his glass and finished the beer. "By late Sunday afternoon your brother finally passed out. He seemed okay at breakfast on Monday, but he had a couple of drinks at lunch."

McCord looked at Clint over the glass. "Mr. Garcia said when they left on Monday afternoon your brother was driving."

For a long time neither man spoke. The waitress came with the chili. McCord said, "Yeah, I'm ready," but Clint waved his away because he knew if he even looked at the simmering mess of beans and meat he'd be sick.

The P.I. swallowed a spoonful of chili, wiped his mouth and said, "After you called last night I got to thinking about your brother's wife. I saw her once in Miami when she was at the Five O'Clock Club. I've never forgotten. She was singing a Gershwin tune...and there was something about her, sadness maybe, a kind of longing in her voice that just about broke my heart." He shrugged. "The lady reached something inside of me, Van Arsdale." He wiped his mouth with the paper napkin. "I'm not especially proud of myself that I told your father what he wanted to hear. Hell, I'd probably do it again. But what I'm telling you now is the truth."

For a long time Clint didn't say anything. Finally he took a pen and a thin black notebook out of his pocket, wrote something, tore out the paper and handed it to McCord. "This is my PO number," he said. "Send your bill there."

"I didn't do this for the money."

"But you'll take it."

McCord grinned. "Yeah. But this time there's a difference. This time I'm doing it right."

Clint drove away from the restaurant without knowing where he was going. He just took the beach road and kept driving. He believed McCord; he accepted the fact that Alan, not Holly, had been driving the day of the accident. He could understand why she had taken the blame. She had loved Alan; she had been loyal to the end.

He could see her doing it. She'd have been in shock, panicked because she knew Alan had been drinking and that he'd probably go to jail. But she'd been badly hurt, losing her baby; how in the hell had she been able to get out of the car, go around, push Alan over and get behind the wheel?

Then, from out of the past, he remembered Gil Loringer, a kid he'd gone to high school with. He and Gil, along with Tony Gutierez and a couple of other guys, drove out to a dirt road on the way to Homosassa Springs to drag race. It was a bright, moonlit night. Gil had a 1956 Chevy he'd spent the summer fixing up; Tony drove his father's '72 Fairlane.

Gil and Tony wanted to be first. While the other guys crawled out of their cars the two of them went barreling down the dark road, tires spitting dirt and gravel, hellbent for leather. Nobody really knew what happened. Maybe Tony hit a rock that threw him into the tree, maybe the two cars jammed together and he lost control. They saw Tony's car veer, heard the crash when it hit the tree and the terrible screech of Gil's brakes.

Four of them piled into his car. He couldn't even remember getting there or he and the other guys jumping out of the car, but he'd never forget the way the car looked smashed up against the tree with its tires spinning and a flash of flame coming out of the hood. Or Gil trying to get the jammed car door open. His face was contorted with effort. They yelled at him, but he didn't hear. Before they could reach him he'd yanked the door right off of its hinges.

"Adrenaline," the doctor said later. "Once I saw a man who'd run over a kid lift a car right up off the ground. Doesn't seem possible, but it happened."

Was that what happened to Holly? Was that how she, herself badly injured, found the strength to lift his unconscious brother from under the steering wheel?

Questions. God, so many questions.

When he finally stopped he pulled off down to a lonely stretch of beach and walked. There were facts he had to face, but it was hard. Alan was his brother; he had loved him. He'd been a holy terror, but there was another side of him, too. A sweeter side. He couldn't drive past a hitchhiker or a hurt animal. He'd stop other cars or if he had to he'd run out in traffic to rescue a wounded coon or a dog.

There wasn't a woman between seventeen and ninety-seven who didn't adore him. When old Annie Pease, who everybody said was the meanest woman in Braxton Beach, fell in her front yard it was Alan who found her, Alan who carried her into her house and stayed with her until the doctor came. He sent flowers and went to visit her every day until she was back on her feet.

He'd slapped Holly.

How did you reconcile the boy, the young man who sent flowers to a mean old lady, to a man who gambled and drank and slapped his wife?

What had happened to the Alan he had known and loved? What had happened to the little boy with the buttercup hair, the boy who had tagged after him, crying, "Wait for me, Clint. Wait for me"?

Clint sat on the sand, head against his knees, thinking about Alan. And about Holly who had worked as a waitress during the day and in whatever sleazy joint she could at night in an effort to keep their heads above water. Holly who had lied to protect his brother. Who had carried and lost his child.

At last Clint stood and walked back to his car. He was tired, down-to-his-bones weary. He wasn't up to a confrontation with his father. Nevertheless, it was time for Jonah to know the truth about Alan.

Chapter Ten

Clint waited until the next morning after breakfast before he approached his father. He'd thought a lot about what he wanted to say, but how to say it was another matter. Jonah had to hear the truth; whether he accepted it was another matter.

His father had never been an easy man. The old adage that people mellow as they grew older didn't apply to him. Jonah hadn't mellowed; if anything he had become more set in his ways, narrower in his opinions, more prejudiced. He still believed that neither blacks nor women should have the right to vote, that anybody with a Spanish name—except for the men and women who worked in his groves—ought to be shipped back across the Mexican border. And that a saloon keeper's daughter should stay on her own side of town.

Clint wondered now as he watched his father sop up half an egg with a spoonful of grits why a woman like his mother, a gentle woman of grace and breeding, had married his father. Perhaps childbirth weakened her, but he had always believed it was the utter despair in her life that killed her.

Clint had been devastated by his mother's death. For months afterward he had dreamed of her at night and he had wanted to die so that he could be with her. His sadness angered his father. One morning at breakfast Jonah had said, "I'm damn tired of your moping, boy. Your mama's dead and that's that. Sitting there sullen ain't going to bring her back. Now you sit up and eat your eggs."

"They're running."

"I don't give a damn if they're galloping. Eat 'em."

"No!" He'd pushed his plate away so hard the eggs slid off the plate onto the white tablecloth. Before he could move, Jonah had pushed back his chair. He grabbed him by the collar, yanked him up out of his chair and slapped him so hard his teeth hurt. "I'm not having any more of your foolishness," he roared. "You straighten up or I'll wallop you so hard you won't sit down for a week."

Alan, frightened and screaming in his high chair, knocked over his glass of milk. When his father turned on the toddler Clint forgot his own hurt. "I'll be good," he cried, putting himself between the baby and his father. "I'm sorry, Papa. I'll eat my eggs. I won't be bad again."

His father never struck him again. Actually, there were times when Clint was growing up that he almost wished Jonah would because that would have meant that Jonah knew he existed. But his father had other things to do with his life. He brought women to the house and often when Clint lay half-asleep in the room he shared with Alan he would hear them, laughing drunkenly as they staggered up the stairs to his father's room.

If his father had a soft spot at all it was for Alan. As the years passed he developed a strong fatherly affection for his younger son. Perhaps in his own way he made an attempt to treat both boys the same, but it was obvious that Alan was the apple of his eye. It devastated him when Alan ran away; it shattered him when Alan was killed.

Clint could understand his father's feelings for he, too, had been shattered by Alan's death. Talking about it now would open an old wound, but perhaps the wound had to be opened in order for it to heal. His father had to know the truth about the accident; he had to know that it hadn't been Holly's fault.

Now, when his father started to push away from the table, Clint said, "Let's have another cup of coffee. There's something I want to talk to you about."

"All right." Jonah sat back down. "And before I forget, you had a call from Dan Goodwin last night."

"Dan called? What did he want?"

"You gotta go on over to Tallahassee today because they've called a special session of the legislature. Got to do with that plan to build a new highway connecting the west coast with the east somewheres up in this part of Florida. They're going to convene on Wednesday and Dan says you and him need to go over some facts and figures before that."

"I'll leave this afternoon."

"You're up for reelection next year." Jonah lighted a cigar and, after he got it glowing the way he wanted, said, "It's time you were thinking about getting married again, Clint. Never could figure out why you left Beth. She was a right smart-looking woman. Good family, plenty of money and good connections because her daddy owned half of Atlanta. Shoulda stayed with her. Don't know why you didn't.''

"She had an affair."

Jonah stared at him. "What're you talking about?"

"She slept with the golf pro at the country club."

"Get outta here! Beth? Pasty-faced, goody-two-shoes Beth? Lord God, who'da thought? Guess you can't tell a book by its cover or a woman by her bloomers."

"No," Clint said, "you can't."

"You got something special on your mind?"

Clint nodded. "I had lunch with McCord yesterday."

"McCord? What'd he want?"

Clint paused, wanting to word this carefully so Jonah wouldn't go sky-high before he had a chance to tell him what he'd learned. He took a sip of his coffee and said, "I called him and asked him to meet me because there were some things I wondered about in the report he gave you."

"Things? What things? You saw the report. No reason you should go behind my back trying to find out something else."

"It wasn't really behind your back, Jonah. I did it because there were still some things I didn't understand." Clint hesitated. "You see, I think McCord wanted to spare you. That's why he—"

"Spare me! What in the hell are you talking about?"

"He's convinced by the evidence he's seen and the people he talked to that Holly wasn't driving when the accident occurred. He's sure Alan was behind the wheel and that he'd probably been drinking."

"That's a damned lie!"

"Alan had been arrested before for driving under the influence. He'd been drinking heavily the weekend it happened. Alan's boss said Alan was driving when he and Holly left Key West to start back to Miami."

"And you believe a cock-and-bull story like that?"

"Yes, I do."

Jonah's face got beet red and his body puffed with outrage. "It's that damn woman!" he shouted. "You believe what McCord says because you probably been shackin' up with her. Got a taste of what your brother married her to get. She's nothing but a—"

"That's enough!" Clint jumped to his feet, fists clenched to his sides.

"Not near enough. What in the hell's the matter with you? She got Alan to run off with her ten years ago so's she could get her hands on my money. Well, I fooled her and I fooled him. Didn't give him a damn cent all the time he was married to her."

"Then it was too late," Clint said. "Then he was dead." He stood and looked down at his father. "But you still had your money, didn't you, Jonah?"

The old man's face mottled with rage. He started up from his chair, yelling, "Don't you talk to me like that. I loved that boy. I would have given him everything I had if he hadn't run off with her. She ruined his life. She—"

"Supported him most of the time."

"Supported him! What're you talking about?"

"Alan drank and he gambled and she had to go to work as a waitress."

"Another damned lie."

"McCord doesn't have any reason to lie."

Jonah glared at him. "No reason? Hellfire, Clint, she's probably been sleeping with him, too."

Clint stiffened. He took a step toward his father, angrier than he'd ever been in his life. It was the closest he'd ever come to hitting the old man. "You're wrong about Holly," he said between clenched teeth. "She's a decent, honorable woman who took the blame for the accident in order to protect Alan."

"She's bamboozled you, boy," Jonah said. "Got you so mixed up you don't hardly know which end is up. She's lying and McCord's lying. Damn shanty Irish saloon girl..."

Clint headed for the door. He'd had enough. One more word about Holly and he wouldn't be able to control himself. "We can talk about this when I get back from Tallahassee," he said. "But I'm telling you now that I'm not going to change my mind about Holly. If I decide she's the woman for me, and if she'll have me in spite of the fact that I'm a Van Arsdale, there isn't a damn thing you can do about it."

Jonah stood where he was for a moment or two after Clint went out. He stared at the closed door. "The hell there isn't," he muttered.

He got out the telephone book, looked up a number, then dialed the phone. When Phoebe Buckaloo answered, he said, "Good morning, Miss Phoebe. This here is Jonah Van Arsdale. Is Buford there? Can I talk to him?"

When Buford came on the line, Jonah said, "I need to see you this afternoon. Got a little something I want you to do for me. How 'bout you come over around two. That okay? Well, then, that's fine. I'll be waiting for you."

When he put the phone down he smiled. Then he picked it up and dialed again.

Clint called Holly just before he left. "I'm on my way to Tallahassee," he said. "I'd like to see you before I go. Can you spare a little time?"

"Yes, I think so. Hattie is here. She'll keep an eye on Aunt Lou."

"Fine. I'll be there in ten minutes."

He made it in five. Holly heard his car in the driveway and hurried out to meet him. "I've missed you," she said when she got into the car.

"And I've missed you." He grinned. "I don't suppose there's any chance of your coming to Tallahassee with me."

Holly shook her head. "I wouldn't feel right about leaving Aunt Lou. How long will you be gone?"

"A few days, maybe a week." He pulled out onto the street and headed for the beach.

The day was overcast; the air was still and so thick with humidity it seemed almost difficult to breathe. It was the end of summer, the beginning of hurricane season. He hoped there wouldn't be one this year. If there was he hoped it wouldn't hit until the orange crop was in. The past few years they'd managed to escape most of the tropical storms. Hurricane Andrew had done a lot of damage on the east coast, but this side of Florida hadn't been too badly hurt.

Hurricane Isabel, back in September of 1960, with winds of more than one hundred and fifty miles an hour, was something else. It knocked down trees and flattened most of the Van Arsdale groves. It had almost wiped his father out.

"Strange weather," Holly said.

"Hurricane season."

"Everything is so still."

"Maybe it'll be cooler down at the beach."

But it wasn't. The water was flat and gray, the air just as muggy. Clint took her hand and when she had taken her shoes off they started walking down the beach. There were almost no people out today, and when Clint saw the slight rise of a dune, he said, "Let's sit down awhile."

He had to tell her about his conversation with Mc-Cord, but it wasn't easy. For a little while he didn't say anything. He looked out at the Gulf, then finally, reaching for her hand, he said, "I told you my father had hired a P.I. to investigate the accident."

"Yes," she said. "You told me."

"I called him yesterday. McCord, the P.I."

Holly's face tightened; she drew her hand away. "You weren't satisfied? You wanted to know more about me? Check me out? See if I—"

"Stop it," he said gently. And when he saw the storm in her eyes he gripped her shoulders and turned her so she would have to look at him. In a low voice, not aware that he had tightened his hold on her, he asked, "Why didn't you tell me that Alan was driving the day of the accident?"

She went still. "How... how did you find out?"

"McCord. He studied the accident pictures. He said Alan could only have sustained the kind of blow to his face that he did if he'd been driving. Why didn't you tell me, Holly?"

"I...I almost did. I started to that day in the kitchen, the day that Aunt Lou took a turn for the worse." Her eyes filled. "I wanted to tell you, Clint. A part of me wanted to, but another part didn't because I know how much you loved Alan. I didn't want to do anything to destroy your memory of him. It was easier for me to..." She stopped, unable to go on.

"To take the blame." He put his arms around her and drew her close. "You should have told me about Alan's drinking and about the gambling, sweetheart. I know

Alan was weak, I could have forgiven him that. What I can't forgive is his striking you."

"How did you know that he—?" She stopped, bottom lip caught between her teeth. And he knew by the expression on her face that it was true.

The thought of it, the thought of his brother striking her, sickened him. He let her go, and clasping his arms around his knees he stared out at the dull, dark water.

"He'd been drinking," Holly said. "He didn't know what he was doing."

Clint couldn't say anything. His face was hard; his eyes were bleak.

"You asked me once to tell you about our marriage, Clint. I think it's time I told you how it was." She waited and when he didn't respond, she said, "At first neither one of us thought very much about the future because every day was a holiday. We didn't mind that we had very little money, that we had to live on peanut butter sandwiches. Those were happy days, Clint. We were so young, so...so innocent."

She moved a little apart from him and began to make small circles in the sand with her fingertip. "When Alan got the job with Island Rum it seemed like everything was perfect. Living was good, living was easy. But then he..."

"Starting drinking," Clint said.

"And gambling. It was like a sickness, Clint. So was the drinking. That's where everything, everything we both earned, went. I got a job singing at night and waiting tables during the day. I didn't mind working, but just to see it...to see it go that way..."

For a little while she didn't say anything, she just kept making those small circles in the sand. Then finally she said, "We went to Puerto Rico. Alan started gambling in the hotel casino. It was almost time for the company banquet to start. Mr. Garcia couldn't find him and so I went back to our room because I knew he'd been drinking and I thought maybe he'd gone up and passed out. I went in..."

She was aware of Clint looking at her now, but she wouldn't look at him. "He... he had a woman in the room, the wife of one of the company men. They were in our bed."

He stared at her, too shocked to speak. He wanted to tell her that his brother wasn't like that, that Alan would never have hurt her that way. But he said nothing; he only waited.

"I left him," she said. "He begged me to come back to him. He told me he'd quit drinking. And so I—"

"You went back to him."

"Yes." She looked at him now. "I went back and I tried, but it wasn't any good. I... I had stopped loving him, Clint. I didn't want to. I tried, but... but it just wasn't there anymore. When I got pregnant I made up my mind that after the baby was born I'd leave him. I think he knew. I think that's why he started drinking again. That was my fault, Clint. My fault because I'd stopped loving him. Maybe if I had tried harder, if I had—"

"No." He cupped her face with his hands. "It wasn't your fault. It wasn't anybody's fault but Alan's." Clint put his arms around her. He felt her tears against his throat and knew she grieved for the young love she had known and lost, and for the baby who had died on that rainy road from Key West.

In a little while he took her back to her aunt's. She looked tired, spent from the ordeal of telling him about Alan. There were so many things he wanted to say to her, but he, too, felt the emotional effect of having at last learned the truth.

"I'll be back in a few days," he said when he walked her to the door. "We'll talk then." He kissed her and for a moment she leaned her face against his shoulder.

When she stepped away from him, she said, "Drive carefully, Clint."

He knew he had to leave, but he didn't want to. It would only be for a few days, yet he was reluctant to be away from her for even that short a time.

He kissed her again, just once, then turned and hurried out to his car.

Late that same afternoon Aunt Lou complained that her hip was so painful she could hardly stand it, so Holly called the doctor. "Probably nothing to worry about," he said. "She's up and around now and it'd be natural she'd have some discomfort. I'll call in a prescription for pain to the drugstore. Give her one of the pills every four hours, that'll make her feel better. Once she's easier try to get her up as often as you can. She needs to start learning how to move her foot and walk again. The pills will help the pain."

When she put the phone down, Holly turned to her aunt and said, "The doctor is going to call in a prescription to Ungerliter's Drugstore. I'll go in and pick it up as soon as I change."

"No," Aunt Lou said. "I'm hurting. You're all right the way you are. Half the women in Braxton Beach run around in shorts during the summer."

"All right. I won't be long."

It was a short walk to town. The air was hot and still, the humidity so thick you could cut it with a bread knife. She waved when she went by Greta Olson's bakery, then went on to the drugstore. The air-conditioning hit her as soon as she opened the door and she could feel her skin cooling when she started back toward the pharmacy.

"Hey," Buford said when she passed the magazine rack. He put the girlie magazine he'd been looking through back. "How's everything?" he asked.

"Fine." She tried to edge past him.

"How's your aunt? Heard she was home from the hospital."

"She's doing all right. I've got to pick up her prescription."

"Sure, you go right ahead. I'm going to make a phone call." He shuffled his feet and, blocking her way, said, "I been wanting to call you to apologize about that morning I came by your house. I wanted to explain and ask your pardon."

When she didn't say anything, he said, "Well... I'll be seein' you."

I hope not, she thought, and pushed past him.

Mr. Ungerliter gave her a smile. "How's Miss Lou doing?" he asked.

"She's been having some pain. The doctor called in a prescription."

"I'm working on it now, Holly. It'll be ready in a minute." He went to the old portable typewriter, probably the same one he'd used for years, and when he'd typed out the instructions, he put it on the bottle, filled the bottle with pills and handed it to her.

"This ought to help," he said. "If you need anything else just give me a call and I'll have it sent over."

"I will, thanks." They chatted a couple of minutes, then she headed back to the front of the store and stopped to buy a *Miami Herald*.

When she waited in line to pay for it, Buford sidled up to her. "What's your hurry?" he asked. "Let's you and me have a soda or something."

"Sorry," she said. "I can't."

"How about a sandwich?"

"No, thank you."

"I guess you're still mad about the way I acted that morning a couple of weeks ago. I haven't hardly been able to live with myself, thinking what I did. Don't know what got into me." He glanced toward the door, then said, "Guess it was seeing you like that, all pretty and fresh. Enough to drive a man crazy." He laughed, then sobered. "But of course that's no excuse for the way I acted and I want to tell you I surely do apologize."

"Apology accepted. Now if you'll excuse me, Buford, I really have to get back to Aunt Lou."

"I'll walk you out."

There wasn't much she could do without making a scene. She went to the door with him, he opened it and when they stepped out onto the sidewalk, he said, "Well, hey, here's old Lucky Bucky. You remember him?"

Buck Willaford had been in the same high school class with her and Buford, but he'd dropped out in the tenth grade. He'd spent the next couple of years in and out of trouble and the last she'd heard he'd been sent to Raiford for stealing cars. She hadn't known him very well and certainly they'd never been friends, but now, all hale and hearty, he threw his arms around her and said, "Holly Moran! How the heck are you? Long time no see."

"Hello, Buck. I'm sorry I can't stop and talk, but I've got to get back to my aunt's house."

He looked at Buford. Buford, hands in his pockets, looked up and down the street as if he was waiting for someone before he turned back to Holly and said, "You ought to be a little more sociable. The three of us went to high school together. We used to be real good friends."

In your dreams, she wanted to say. But didn't.

"I hear you been living in New Orleans," Buck said. "That's some kind of town. Went there two years ago for Mardi Gras and had me a high old time. Drank a dozen of them hurricane drinks at Pat O'Brien's." He glanced out at the passing cars, raised his eyebrows at Buford, then put his arm around Holly's waist. "But I bet I coulda had a better time if you'd been there to show me around."

Holly tried to step away, but when she did Buck tightened his arm around her.

"I got a hunch the three of us could have a real good time right here in Braxton Beach," he said. "You 'n' me and old Buford here."

Buford grinned and stepped closer, blocking her escape.

Holly said, "Please, let me go." She looked up and down the sidewalk for help, but except for a few cars there was no one in sight. Everybody was staying in this afternoon because of the heat. Suddenly she saw a sheriff's car coming fast around the corner toward them. She raised her hand to try to signal and to her relief it screeched to a stop. The sheriff stepped out. "What's going on here?" he yelled.

"Nothing." Buck let Holly go.

"Whad'ya mean nothing? Sure looks like something to me."

Holly took a step forward, but before she could say anything, Buford said, "Tell you the truth, Sheriff Teasdale, Holly here was propositioning us."

"What?" Her eyes went wide with shock.

"You sure?" the sheriff asked.

"Well, yeah." Buck shuffled his feet and looked embarrassed. "We were just funning around because we've known Holly since back in high school. Didn't know she'd turned pro."

"What are you talking about?" Holly cried.

The sheriff turned to Buford. "He telling the truth?"

"'Fraid so, Sheriff." Buford looked sadly at Holly and shook his head. "I guess you just never know about people. She said she'd take us both on for a hundred dollars. Said she usually got two hundred in New Orleans but that this'd be for old time's sake."

"You're lying!" She couldn't believe this was happening.

People inside the drugstore came out and stood in a group watching them. She caught a glimpse of Mr. Ungerliter. She said, "My God, Buford! Why are you doing this? It isn't funny. It—"

"Keep your voice down, young lady," the sheriff said. "You're in enough trouble as it is."

"Trouble? But I haven't done anything."

"Way I see it you been soliciting and now you're disturbing the peace. That's plenty of trouble."

"But—"

He grabbed her, yanked her around, pulled her hands behind her back and cuffed her.

"Buford," she said. "Buford, please. Tell him the truth."

When he grinned she saw the meanness in his eyes. "Already have," he said.

Teasdale headed her toward the car, opened the back door and shoved her in. She said, "Wait a minute. Wait..." And he slammed the door.

He went around the squad car, got in and, with siren wailing, headed for the station.

Dear God. This couldn't be happening. What was this all about? What was the sheriff going to do to her?

Chapter Eleven

The next couple of hours went by so fast Holly couldn't keep up. She was hustled into the station and made to sit on a wooden bench until a uniformed man said, "Come along, miss." He took the cuffs off and fingerprinted her. A different deputy shoved her over in front of a screen and made her stand there while he took her picture, front and sideways.

When she said, "I want to make a phone call," he winked at the man who'd fingerprinted her and said, "Phone ain't workin', is it, Billy?"

The man named Billy looked uncomfortable. He was older than the other two deputies in the room, bald, anxious looking. "Sheriff Teasdale," he started to say, "Sheriff, I don't think we—"

"Shut your mouth!" the sheriff snapped, and the man turned away.

"I have the right to make a call and to see an attorney," Holly said, forcing herself to be calm.

"Whooee," the man who'd winked said. He was tall and skinny as a whooping crane. "Would you listen to this gal?" he said. "Must think she's in the big city where they got them spit 'n' polish *po*-lice."

"Reckon she's going to find out how we handle things here, Bobby Joe," the sheriff said. "Billy, I want you should start the paperwork while Bobby Joe goes through her purse. And you, missy, you stand right there like a good girl."

"You can't do this!" Holly protested, raising her voice. "I haven't done anything. Buck and Buford were lying. You can't honestly believe that I...that I'm a prostitute. That's ridiculous. You've got to let me call my father."

"I don't have to let you do anything. Anyway, the phone don't work."

"You can't do this."

He stuck his face up close to hers. "I can do anything I damn please," he said. "So you stand there until I tell you to move. You hear?"

She bit back a retort and, though it cost her, did as she was told.

The contents of her purse were turned upside down on a desk. Bobby Joe pawed through her things. "Aha!" he said. "Lookee what we got here, Sheriff. Bottle of pills. Looks to me like some kind of illegal drug."

"The pills are for my aunt," Holly said. "They're a prescription."

"Uh-huh." Teasdale shook his head. "Well, we'll just send them on over to the lab and see. That'll take a few days, maybe a week. I reckon we'll just have to keep you locked up till we know for sure."

"You can call Mr. Ungerliter," Holly said. "He'll tell you what they are."

"You trying to tell me how to do my job?"

No, she thought, but somebody should. This was a nightmare; it couldn't be happening. Her mouth was dry, her heart beating so hard that for a moment she thought she was going to faint.

The man who'd been going through the things in her purse stuffed them back inside. "Maybe we should have her searched, boss."

"Part of the regulations," Teasdale said with a smirk.

Bobby Joe said, "The judge is waiting for you, Sheriff. I reckon you'll have to search her later."

"You can't deny me the right to make a call," Holly said. "I demand—"

"Lord'a mercy," Bobby Joe said. "She's demanding. Don't that scare you?"

Teasdale grabbed her wrists and cuffed them. The phone started ringing as he shoved her out into the hall.

They went to a door marked Judge Elmer P. Smith. Teasdale knocked and took her in. The man behind a weather-beaten desk said, "This her?"

"Yep. Caught her soliciting a couple of our local boys. Seems to me like we ought to make an example of her."

"Seems like." Elmer P. Smith shifted a wad of tobacco from one cheek to the other, then spat into a brass-plated spittoon. "You got the paperwork?"

"Right here, Judge."

Smith gave it only a cursory glance. "Okay." He picked up a gavel and banged it on the desk. "Thirty days at the prison work farm, your lady." He squinted up at the sheriff. "Iffen I was you I'd hustle her right on over there."

"Plan to." Teasdale grabbed Holly's shoulder. She stiffened. "You can't do this," she protested. "I have the right to—"

"You don't have any rights a'tall." Judge Smith glared at her. And to Sheriff Teasdale, he said, "Get her out of here."

The man was a poor excuse for a judge, probably appointed because he'd done somebody a political favor. She'd been set up. But by who? Surely Buford, even though he might still be angry about Clint's throwing him out of her house, didn't have enough influence to have arranged this. He might be one of the "good old boys" who did favors for other, more powerful men, but—

More powerful men. The breath stopped in Holly's throat because suddenly she knew with a certainty that sickened her that Jonah Van Arsdale had set this up. He hated her enough; he was powerful enough to have done it.

Teasdale grabbed her manacled hands and gave her a shove. She panicked, crying, "No! Don't do this. You can't! Oh, please—"

But Teasdale didn't listen. He just pushed her out the door and headed for his patrol car.

The phone was ringing when Rosie O'Toole started up the stairs to Lou's. She knocked, heard Hattie call out, "Just a minute," and waited. When Hattie came to the door she said, "Something's happened to Miss Holly."

"What are you talking about?"

"It's Mr. Ungerliter on the phone. Maybe you'd better talk to him."

Rosie hurried into the house. She went past Lou, said, "Afternoon, Miss Lou," and reached for the phone.

"Hello? Ungerliter? This is Rosie O'Toole. What's going on? Hattie said..." She listened, then shook her head. "You must be mistaken. Are you sure it was Holly? How long ago? Yes, yes, all right. Thanks for calling."

"What is it?" Lou looked frightened. "Has something happened to Holly? Is she hurt? What is it?"

"She's not hurt, but..." Rosie paused and shook her head. "There has to have been some mistake."

"What kind of a mistake? What are you talking about? What's happened to Holly?"

"She's been arrested!"

All the color faded from Aunt Lou's face. "She couldn't have been. What for?" She started to tremble. "Oh, Lord. Oh, my sweet Lord. We've got to do something. Call Pat. He'll know what to do."

Rosie reached for the phone, dialed the number of the Dirty Shame and let it ring. There was no answer. She looked at her watch. "Damn," he said, "he isn't there yet."

"Call him at home."

Rosie did. There was no answer there, either. "Who's your lawyer?" she asked Lou.

"Alex Harwood."

"What's his number?"

"It's in the little red book on the table by my bed."

Rosie ran in to get it. "Harwood," she said under her breath. "Harwood."

She found the number and dialed it. A woman answered. Rosie said, "Let me talk to Mr. Harwood."

"I'm sorry. He isn't here."

"This is an emergency. Where can I reach him."

"He's out of town until next Wednesday."

"Damn!"

"I beg your pardon? Who shall I say—"

But Rosie had already hung up.

Hattie was wringing her hands; Aunt Lou started to cry. Rosie said, "Let me think. Let me think."

She had to do something. But what?

Clint had left for Tallahassee later than he'd intended. But it didn't matter, he was glad he'd spent the time with Holly and that he had told her about talking to McCord. She'd finally opened up about her marriage to Alan, and although it had been hard to hear, he was grateful that she trusted him enough to tell him the way it had been.

She'd had a rough time; he hoped that in some way he could make it up to her. As for Alan, he would try to remember the good things about him, remember him as he had been when he was a boy because right now he couldn't stand to think of the man he had become.

There was a lot of traffic, but in another couple of minutes he'd be on 75. Then, although it was still a three-hour drive, it was a straight shot to Tallahassee.

His car phone rang about a mile before he would hit the interstate. He picked it up, said, "Yes? Hello?"

A voice he wasn't familiar with said, "Mr. Van Arsdale?"

"Yes, who is this?"

"It's Rosie O'Toole, Mr. Van Arsdale. Miss Lou's nurse from the hospital."

He knew right away that something was wrong. Was it Holly's aunt? Had something happened to her? "Is it Miss Lou?"

"No, sir. It's Holly. She's been arrested."

"Arrested?" The car swerved. "What in the hell are you talking about? What for?"

"I don't know. All I know is that Mr. Ungerliter, he's the pharmacist at the drugstore, called and said there was some kind of commotion in front of the store. He got there just as the sheriff handcuffed Holly and took her away. I didn't know what else to do, Mr. Van Arsdale. I couldn't get Holly's father or her lawyer so I called your house. A maid there told me you were on your way to Tallahassee. Then I remembered your car phone number from when you took Holly to dinner. I hope that's all right."

"Of course it's all right. Hold on." He slowed the car, pulled to the side, made a U-turn and started back the way he'd come. "I'm about thirty miles out of town," he said. "I'm on my way."

He hung up and dialed the governor's office in Tallahassee. When Sarah Jane Wintz, the governor's secretary, answered, he said, "This is Senator Van Arsdale. I'm calling from my car phone. It's urgent. Can you put me through to the governor?"

"Of course, Mr. Van Arsdale. Please hold on."

He waited. The governor came on the line. "Hey, Clint," he said. "You on your way here?"

"I was, Governor, but I've got an emergency and I've just turned back."

"Not your dad, is it?"

"No, sir. It's something about a friend of mine. She's in trouble. Apparently she's been picked up by our local sheriff and arrested."

"What's the charge?"

"I have no idea."

"How can I help?"

"I need some kind of authorization from your office, something that will give me the right to interfere if I have to." Clint hesitated. "The sheriff is a real redneck, George. A throwback to the kind of small-town cops that scared the hell out of the blacks and damn near everybody else in the fifties. He's got no business being in office.''

''Okay, Clint, I understand. You tell him you're acting on my behalf as a special deputy of the attorney general's office. He gives you any trouble you tell him to phone me.''

''Thanks, George.''

''Let me know what happens.''

''I will. Goodbye.''

Clint put the phone down. Then he hit the accelerator, got it up to eighty and kept it there.

They led Holly toward the back of the jail. She was scared to death, so frightened she thought she was going to be sick. In spite of the heat she was cold, shivering as though with a chill. Her wrists hurt from the handcuffs, and every time the sheriff grabbed them a streak of pain shot through her.

She kept thinking this couldn't be happening, that it was a dream, a terrible nightmare, and that any minute now she was going to wake up. Nothing like this had ever happened to her before. It wasn't real. Please, God, she prayed, don't let it be real.

Teasdale shoved Holly ahead of him, down a long, gray hall toward a door at the far end. She panicked when she saw it and tried to jerk away. He jerked her back, yanked on the cuffs that bound her and she cried out.

They reached the door. She saw the sheriff's car in the parking lot, the wire screen separating the back seat from the front. She struggled, not caring that her wrists hurt. The deputy grabbed her shoulder and pushed her forward. The sheriff opened the rear door.

"Shove her in, B.J.," he said. "I want to get her out of here as quick as I—" He stopped. A big black car swung into the parking lot and screeched to a stop.

"What the hell!" Bobby Joe said.

Clint jumped out. "Stop right there!" he called out.

Bobby Joe reached for his gun, but before he could pull it out of his holster, Teasdale said, "No! Wait! That's Clint Van Arsdale."

Clint ran forward. "Are you all right?" he asked Holly.

She went weak with relief. Clint was here; he'd know what to do.

"What happened?"

"He...he arrested me," she said, indicating the sheriff. "He's taking me to the prison farm."

"He's not taking you anywhere." He turned to Teasdale. "Take those cuffs off," he ordered.

"Now wait just a damn minute, Clint. You can't come in here and interfere with me this way."

"The hell I can't! I've spoken to the governor and I have authorization for her release. Uncuff her."

"He can't do this, can he?" Bobby Joe asked.

Teasdale didn't bother answering. To Clint he said, "You got some kind of an official paper or something?"

"No."

"Then get out of my way."

Clint reached inside his car, took the phone, dialed and when it was answered said, "Sarah Jane, this is Senator Van Arsdale again. Please let me speak to the governor."

"No need to do that, Clint." Teasdale's face got red. "Maybe there's been some kind of a mistake."

"There's a mistake all right," Clint said. "And you're it." He turned to Holly. "Did anybody read you your rights?" he asked. "Were you allowed to make a phone call or speak to an attorney?"

"No, they didn't read me my rights. They wouldn't let me call anybody."

He turned back to the phone. "Governor?" he said. "I'm in Braxton Beach. The sheriff here, a man named Henry Teasdale, is about to take a Holly Moran to the prison farm. She wasn't Mirandaized or allowed to make a phone call or talk to a lawyer. I've asked Mr. Teasdale to release her, but he has refused." He listened a moment, said, "Of course," and handed the phone to the sheriff.

Teasdale said, "Uh, Governor..." He listened and the color slowly faded from his face. "I . . . I understand. Yes, sir. Of course, sir. I'll . . . I'll turn her over to the senator. Right away, sir." He was sweating when he handed the phone back to Clint.

"Thank you, Governor," Clint said, and hung up.

Teasdale took his keys out of his pocket. His hands were shaking. He dropped them. Bobby Joe picked them up. He looked as if he wanted to say something. The sheriff opened his mouth a couple of times, but nothing came out.

The sheriff unlocked the handcuffs. He said, "This is just a misunderstanding, Mr. Van Arsdale. If I'da known Holly was a special friend of yours—"

"Shut up." Clint put his arm around Holly. "Are you all right?" he asked. "Did they hurt you?"

She shook her head, almost too weak with relief to stand. "But I was so frightened. They talked about strip-searching me."

Clint stiffened. She felt his shoulder muscles bunch. "Get in the car," he said.

"Clint...don't, don't do anything. Not now. I just want to get away from here. Please."

He hesitated. But then he took her arm and helped her into his car. When he closed the door he turned back to the sheriff and his deputy. "I don't know what went on here today," he said to Teasdale. "But I'm going to find out. What you did to Miss Moran was illegal and it's going to cost you your badge."

"Now hold on, Clint. You can't do that. You can't—"

But Clint had already started backing out of the lot.

He headed for the beach and when they reached it he stopped, facing the water. He didn't say anything, he just put his arms around Holly and held her.

"You're safe now, sweetheart," he said. "It's all over."

"It was so awful. I was so scared."

He held her away from him. "What happened, Holly? What was it all about?"

She took a deep breath and forced herself to speak calmly. "I went to the drugstore to pick up a prescription for Aunt Lou. Buford saw me when I went in. He talked to me, but I brushed him off and went to get the prescription and he...said he had to make a phone call. He was waiting for me when I came back from the prescription counter and insisted on leaving the store with me. Buck Willaford was waiting outside the store."

"Buck? I didn't know he was out of Raiford." Clint took her hand. "Go on," he said. "What happened then?"

"We talked for a couple of minutes. It was strange—they kept looking up and down the street. When I said I had to go, Buck put his arm around me. I tried to get away. Then Buford stepped in front of me and ... and then the sheriff drove up. He wanted to know what was going on and Buck told him ... told him I ... that I had been sol ... soliciting them and Buford said he didn't know that I turned pro and I ..." She covered her face with her hands, unable to go on.

Clint pulled her closer. "It's over," he said gently.

But the expression on his face was anything but gentle. He looked murderous, ready to kill both Buford Buckaloo and Buck Willaford. It was probably Buckaloo who'd set it up to get even with Holly for that Saturday morning she'd spurned him, the morning he'd thrown Buford down her back steps. He wished he'd beaten the hell out of him then, and knew that now he would.

He kissed the top of Holly's head and held her for a little while without speaking. He took her hand, and when he saw how red her wrists were, he cursed under his breath. And vowed that he would get Buford and Buck and the sheriff. And anyone else who'd had anything to do with Holly's arrest.

She raised her face so that she could look at him. "How did you know what had happened?" she asked.

"Rosie O'Toole called me on the car phone. Mr. Ungerliter had called her. She'd tried to reach your dad. When she couldn't get him she tried Alex Harwood, but he was out of town. Finally she called me." He brushed the hair back from Holly's face. "Thank God she did," he said.

He wanted to take her someplace where they could be alone, where he could hold her. But he knew her aunt was worried; he had to get her home.

"Your aunt is probably going out of her mind," he said. "I've got to take you home."

"Yes, she must be frantic."

He started the car and headed for Miss Lou's. As soon as he pulled into the driveway Rosie O'Toole ran down the front steps. She opened the door on Holly's side and, taking her arm, helped her out. "Are you all right?" she said. "We were so worried. Your aunt is beside herself and your dad's on his way over."

She turned to say hello to Clint. He said, "Thank you for calling me. If you hadn't..." No, he didn't want to think about that, about Holly at the prison farm. She was safe now and he planned to keep her that way.

He put his arm around her and, with Rosie on the other side, they went into the house.

"Holly!" Aunt Lou held out her arms and started to cry. "Oh, Holly."

Holly ran across the room and knelt beside her aunt's chair. She put her arms around her waist and held her. "I'm all right," she said. "Don't cry. Don't cry."

Clint felt a knot rise in his throat. Beside him, Rosie said, "Thank God I was able to reach you."

"Yes," he said. "Thank God."

Pat Moran came running up the steps of the house. "Holly, darlin'," he cried. "What happened? Rosie told me you'd been arrested. Are you all right?"

She rose. "Yes, Dad."

He put his arms around her, and over her shoulder he looked at Clint and said, "Rosie called me. Thank you for gettin' her free, Clint."

Clint nodded. Holly was safe now, here with her family. He had a couple of things to do that wouldn't wait.

"I've got to go," he said.

Holly stepped away from her father. "Back to Tallahassee?"

He shook his head. "I'll put it off for a day or two. There's something I want to take care of first."

"Buford," she said.

He nodded.

"Clint . . . I . . . don't think it was—"

But he cut her off. "I'll call the attorney general's office," he said. "I want to get an investigation started here before I go to Tallahassee." He put his hands on her shoulders. "When I go, Holly, I want you to come with me."

Her eyes widened. She looked at him, at her father, then at Aunt Lou. "Clint," she said. "I . . . I don't know. I—"

"That sounds like a real good idea," Rosie said. "Do you the world of good to get away for a few days. Forget all about today."

"Well, I . . ."

"Tallahassee's a real nice place," Aunt Lou said. "Miss O'Toole is right, you need to get away for a few days." She looked at her brother-in-law. "Do her good, don't you think, Pat?"

He cleared his throat. "I guess it'd be all right."

"Then it's settled," Rosie O'Toole said, taking charge. "Mr. Van Arsdale will do whatever it is he has to do and then he and Holly will go on to Tallahassee for a few days. Pat and I and Hattie will take care of Miss Lou.''

It seemed to be settled and for the first time during this long and terrible afternoon Holly was able to smile. She went to the door with Clint and kissed him goodbye.

''I'll be over sometime tonight.'' He held her for a moment before he let her go. Then he hurried out to his car and headed for Buford Buckaloo's.

Chapter Twelve

Clint drove directly to the Buckaloo house. When Phoebe Buckaloo answered the door he didn't waste time on preliminaries. "Where's Buford?" he asked.

She came out onto the porch, wiping her hands on her apron. "He and Buck Willaford took off fishing this afternoon, Mr. Van Arsdale."

"Where?"

"Is something wrong?"

"Where did they go, Mrs. Buckaloo?"

"I'm not real sure. How come you want to know?"

"I have to talk to Buford."

"He'll be back in two or three days."

"That's not soon enough."

She looked upset, a little frightened, before she turned and yelled, "Wilbur? Come on out here, Wilbur."

Her husband, newspaper in his hand, glasses down over the bridge of his nose, came to the door. "Evenin',

Clint," he said. "What're you standing out there for? Come on in."

"I can't right now. I'm looking for Buford. Mrs. Buckaloo said he'd gone fishing. Do you know where?"

"Seems to me he said something about going on over toward Tarpon Springs. Is there something I can help you with?"

"Do you have any idea where he might be staying there?"

"'Fraid not." Buckaloo took his glasses off and rubbed the bridge of his nose. "He isn't in any trouble, is he?"

Clint's mouth tightened. "He will be as soon as I get hold of him."

"What are you talking about?" Phoebe asked. "What kind of trouble? Buford's a good boy. He wouldn't—"

"Dammit to hell!" Wilbur exploded, cutting her off. "I knew something would happen when he started running around with Buck again." He stepped out onto the porch. "What's going on, Clint? What did Buford do?"

"He and Buck ganged up on Holly Moran today when she came out of Ungerliter's Drugstore. The sheriff happened by and when he stopped they told him that Holly has been . . ." Clint struggled for the word, took a deep breath and said, "Soliciting."

"For what?" Wilbur looked puzzled. "I don't know what you mean, Clint. Was she selling something? Getting up a petition? What're you talking about?"

"Prostitution," Clint said. "They accused her of soliciting for the purpose of prostitution."

The other man stared at him. "Holly? Get outta here! That's the most ridiculous thing I've ever heard. Nice girl like that. Maybe they thought they were having some fun with her, joking around. But it certainly wasn't funny, not with somebody as nice as Holly Moran.''

"Humph!" Phoebe, hands on her hips, looking as sour as an unripe persimmon, said, "Nice! Everybody in town knows what kind she is and so should you, Clint. Run off with your own brother and was responsible for killing him in that accident. Been singing and God only knows what else over in New Orleans. Whatever trouble she's in doesn't have a thing to do with Buford. He wouldn't have anything to do with a woman like her. Why she's—''

"That's enough!" Wilbur's cheeks were pink. "Get back in the house."

"Don't you let him say anything bad about Buford."

"Get in the house!" he yelled.

"Seems to me you'd be standing up for your own son, not defending the likes of Holly Moran." With that she went in and banged the screen door behind her.

Wilbur Buckaloo looked at Clint and shook his head. "She's not an easy woman." He indicated the porch chairs. "Let's sit down for a minute while you tell me what this is all about."

Clint talked and Wilbur listened.

When Clint finished the older man said, "Is what happened today serious enough to get him arrested?"

"I don't know," Clint said truthfully. "Even if it is I want to get my hands on him first."

"Don't blame you." Wilbur massaged the bridge of his nose. "Strange," he said. "Even if Buford and Buck said that about Holly you'd think Sheriff Teasdale would have had sense enough to know it wasn't so. Real odd, him coming along just when they were bothering her."

"Yes, it is. But to tell you the truth, Mr. Buckaloo, I'm so damn mad about this that I haven't had a chance to sit down and think things through."

"Don't blame you, Clint. Listen, tell you what I'll do. First thing in the morning I'll go on over to Tarpon Springs and haul Buford back here and turn him over to you."

Clint nodded. "Thanks, Buckaloo," he said. "Call me if you find him."

"I will, Clint. You got my word on it." Wilbur offered his hand. Clint shook it. And wondered how a man as decent as Wilbur Buckaloo had ended up with a wife like Phoebe and a son like Buford.

Holly stayed in the shower for a long time that night. She scrubbed her skin and washed her hair, then stood under the hot water to try to rinse away the fear and horror she'd felt that afternoon. She didn't remember ever having been that frightened, that helpless. That had been the worst, her terrible feeling of helplessness. If it hadn't been for Clint the sheriff would have taken her to the prison farm. She didn't know how she would have survived that.

When she got out of the shower, and after she had dried her hair, she put on pants and a long-sleeved cotton shirt to hide her bruised wrists.

Rosie had supper ready. Pat was there. He said Murph O'Brien was going to open the Dirty Shame. He'd go over later.

"I called the attorney general's office in Tallahassee," he told Holly when she sat down at the table. "They already knew something about what happened to you from Clint. They're goin' to investigate."

"Well, something should certainly be done," Aunt Lou said. "Imagine the sheriff arresting Holly. He ought to lose his badge."

"He will if Clint's got anything to do," Pat commented. "I got a feeling all hell's going to break loose." He reached for a piece of fried chicken. "Clint's a good man, and, Rosie, I want to thank you for having sense enough to call him when you couldn't get me."

"It's probably just as well I couldn't get you," the nurse said. "I'm afraid you'd have torn the sheriff's office apart."

"I still might. I always knew Teasdale wasn't much of a sheriff and it beats the heck out of me how come he's been in office for eight years. He hasn't hardly sense enough to come in out of the rain. And that deputy of his! What's his name? Bobby Joe? He's even dumber than Teasdale and, what's worse, he's rattlesnake mean."

Pat stopped long enough to take a drink of buttermilk. "He and Teasdale are a pair. Makes me sick to my stomach thinkin' about Holly bein' in the same room with the two of them. I'm mighty grateful to Clint for rushing back here the way he did when Rosie called him."

"He's a real good man," Aunt Lou said.

"That he is." Pat turned to Holly. "I don't doubt for a minute that he's fond of you, but . . ." He stopped to take a helping of mashed potatoes. "But I can't say that I approve of you going off to Tallahassee with him. One thing could lead to another—"

"That's the way it usually works," Rosie said.

He started to frown, then across the table he met her gaze. Color rushed into his cheeks; he had a sheepish grin on his face.

Aunt Lou looked at Holly and raised her eyebrows. And Holly thought, Good heavens, they're having an affair. She felt the rise of a laugh and quickly stopped it. Her dad was almost sixty, old enough to make his own decisions. Rosie O'Toole might not be the kind of woman she'd envisioned for him, but if Rosie made him happy, then it was all right with her. He was a dear and a loving man; she wanted him to be happy.

The phone rang then, interrupting her thoughts. Pat said, "I'll get it," and hurried to answer. He said, "Oh, hello, Clint. You did? Did you find him? Well, both he and Buck have got to come back sometime and when they do the two of us will pay them a visit. Hang on a minute, I'll let you talk to Holly."

"Hi," she said when Pat handed her the phone. "We're just having dinner. Fried chicken. Are you coming over?"

"A little later," he said. "I imagine you're tired."

"Not too tired to see you."

"It'll be an hour or so."

"All right, Clint. Goodbye."

"He went looking for Buford," Pat said when Holly came back to the table. "Buford wasn't home. Seems like he and Buck Willaford left town the minute the sheriff took Holly away."

"They'll be back," Aunt Lou said.

"They're going to be in trouble when they do." Rosie passed more chicken to Pat. "Your dad told me you'd had trouble with Buford before, Holly."

"Yes, he came by one morning while Aunt Lou was in the hospital. It was a bad situation. I was struggling to get away from him, actually I was so frightened I screamed. Clint had just walked around the back of the house when he heard me. He grabbed Buford and threw him out the door.''

"Do you think that's why Buford did what he did today? To get even with you?''

"Maybe. But I honestly don't think he'd have enough clout, or enough brains for that matter, to set it up, to arrange it with the sheriff and with the judge.''

Pat paused, the fork halfway to his mouth. "Then if he didn't, who did?''

"Somebody with influence.'' Holly looked across the table at her father, her gaze level with his. "A man powerful enough to pull a few strings. A man who always gets what he wants.''

"Holy Mother.'' Pat put his fork down. He took another drink of buttermilk, wiped off the white mustache it made with his napkin and said, "That'll make it difficult for you, won't it, lass?''

"Yes, Dad. If what I think is true, it's going to be difficult.''

"What are you talking about?'' Aunt Lou asked.

"Holly's only guessing at somethin','' Pat said. "Until she's sure maybe it's better we don't talk about it.'' And to Holly, he said, "Maybe it's a good idea, after all, you're going on over to Tallahassee with Clint. Give the two of you time to talk.'' He reached over and patted her hand. "It won't be easy,'' he said.

"No, it won't be easy.''

She finished the rest of the meal in silence.

Her father and Rosie were gone and her aunt was in bed by the time Clint returned that night. She had undressed earlier and was wearing pajamas and the yellow terry-cloth robe when he arrived.

He kissed her, and when she started into the living room, he said, "Can we go out to the kitchen instead?"

It was his favorite room in the house, a warm and comforting room where he could relax and feel at peace. He wanted to sit there again with Holly, to drink coffee with her, to hold her hand and know that she was safe.

The two cats blinked sleepy eyes when Holly turned a lamp on, then rose and wound themselves around her legs. "You've had enough to eat," she said, then relenting, opened the refrigerator and gave them each a bite of leftover chicken.

"Coffee?" she asked Clint.

"Yes, please." He pulled a chair out from the table and watched her as she prepared it. Her movements were fluid, graceful. She was, he thought, the most feminine of women, with all a woman's strength and fragility. That she had been arrested, handcuffed, then threatened while the sheriff stood by made him almost physically ill.

When she returned with their coffee and a plate of cookies, he reached for her hand. "Are you all right?" he asked. "Did they..." He saw her wrist. It was still red from the manacles and starting to bruise. He took her other wrist and, wrapping his fingers around both, gently rubbed them.

"I'm so sorry this happened," he said in a low voice. "I couldn't believe it when Rosie O'Toole called me. How could you have been arrested?" He shook his head. "I don't understand, but I know I've never been so angry, Holly. I wanted to kill Teasdale today. What in the hell was the matter with him, believing a couple of losers like Buck and Buford? I know he's a poor excuse for a sheriff, but why would he take their word over yours?"

Tell him, a voice inside her head whispered. Tell him what you suspect. But she couldn't, not yet.

"And Judge Smith," Clint went on. "He's a senile old coot, but senile or not, he should have been smart enough to release you. Instead he sentenced you to thirty days at the prison farm."

Clint got up and began to pace. "I'm damned if I understand how or why this could have happened."

"Sit down," she said. "Finish your coffee. It's over, thanks to you. I don't think the sheriff will bother me again."

When he sat down he pulled her up onto his lap. He rested his face against hers and held her without speaking.

She stroked the hair back from his forehead and kissed his brow, holding him as he held her. The fear she'd known earlier today faded; she was safe here in his arms.

"You'll come to Tallahassee with me?" he asked.

"If that's what you want."

He tightened his arms around her. "That's what I want."

"When?"

"The day after tomorrow. I have to be there for a meeting. It may take a day or two. After that we'll drive down to Miami for a few days, or maybe fly over to one of the islands. Would you like that?"

"With you?" She smiled. "Of course I would, if you can spare the time."

"I can and I will."

Nurse O'Toole would look in on Miss Lou, and Hattie could move in to stay nights while they were away. She'd had a bad experience; she needed to get away.

Clint nuzzled her neck and wished he could carry her upstairs to her bed. Tonight of all nights he felt such a need to hold and comfort her without any thought of making love. Only then could he assure himself that she was safe.

But as much as he wanted to be with her tonight he knew he couldn't. This was Miss Lou's house; she wouldn't approve.

He kissed her gently, without passion. And thought about how it would be when they were alone in his home in Tallahassee.

That afternoon an attorney from the governor's office came to talk to Holly.

It occurred to her to wonder why all this fuss was being made. Yes, she had been falsely accused and arrested, but surely there had been false arrests before that had never received this kind of attention. It was because of Clint, of course, because he was a state senator and angry enough to raise hell, determined to get to the bottom of why she had been arrested. And when he did? When he found out who was responsible for her arrest what would he do? What if her suspicions about his father were true? How that would hurt him.

For a moment the thought came that if she could she would stop this before it went any further. Because of Clint. Because she didn't want to hurt him.

The attorney introduced herself as Miss Jane Bueller. She asked if Holly minded her using a tape recorder and when Holly said no the woman switched it on.

She asked Holly about the circumstances of her arrest. She raised her eyebrows when Holly told her the charge had been prostitution. She noted Buford's address and the name of the rooming house where Buck

Willaford boarded. She asked Holly if, when she had been arrested, she had been read her rights. Holly said no. Had she been allowed to make a phone call?

"No," Holly said. "When I asked to I was told the phone was out of order. It rang a few minutes later so I knew the men in the sheriff's office were lying."

"It's easy enough to check that out with the telephone company," the other woman said. "Were you told you could consult an attorney?"

"No. I asked for one and they laughed at me. One of the deputies—they called him Billy—tried to object to the way I was being treated. The sheriff told him to shut up."

The attorney noted the name, then continued, "After that you were taken before Judge..." She consulted her notes. "Elmer P. Smith?"

"That's right. I tried to protest. I told him I hadn't been allowed to make a phone call or consult a lawyer."

"What did he say?"

"That I shouldn't tell him about the law."

"I see." Bueller snapped the tape recorder off. Holly was given a paper to sign, verifying that everything she said was true.

"What do you think will happen now?" Holly asked.

"I don't know what will happen to the two men who falsely accused you, but I think Sheriff Teasdale will be relieved of his duties and Judge Smith will be asked to step down from the bench. Also, because this happened in Senator Van Arsdale's hometown, I think it likely that the governor will appoint an investigative committee to find out how this whole thing was set up."

An investigative committee. How far would it go? Would they discover what she already suspected, that Jonah was responsible for her false arrest? And if they did, what would that mean to Clint? And to their relationship?

Jonah Van Arsdale might be a mean, vindictive man, but he was Clint's father. If the truth came out, would he stand by his father against her?

She took Miss Bueller to the door and thanked her for coming. Then she went upstairs to pack for her trip to Tallahassee.

Chapter Thirteen

They spoke very little on the drive to Tallahassee, so involved were they in their own thoughts. He held her hand when he could and when, because of traffic, he couldn't, she rested a hand on his thigh.

She hoped now that nothing would come from the investigation into her arrest and she almost wished she hadn't spoken to the woman from the attorney general's office. She was free, what good would come from an investigation that might involve Clint's father? In a few weeks she would leave Braxton Beach to go back to New Orleans, unless ... She turned to study Clint's face. He looked intent, solemn, and she wondered if, when the time came and she told him she was leaving, he would ask her to stay. And what she would do if he did.

She sighed then and he said, "Tired, Holly?"

"Just a little."

"Didn't you sleep well last night?"

No, she wanted to say. Every time I closed my eyes I was back in the sheriff's office. And because she didn't want to talk about it, she said, "I'd have slept a lot better if you had been with me."

He drew her closer. "So would I," he said. "But we'll be together tonight."

With the thought of it, of how it would be when she was in his arms again, Clint pressed his foot down on the accelerator, and when she laughed and said, "Slow down, we want to get there all in one piece," he laughed with her and slowed to a respectable sixty-five.

Because they had been late leaving Braxton Beach, it was early evening by the time they reached Tallahassee. Clint's house, white with brick-colored shutters, was on a quiet tree-lined street a few blocks from the state capitol. It sat back from the street, shaded by red maples and a huge live oak hung with Spanish moss.

He pulled into the circular driveway, and when he stopped, the front door opened and a middle-aged woman, wearing a gray uniform and a white apron smiled and stepped out onto the wide front porch.

Clint got out and hurried to open Holly's door before he said, "Evening, Mildred."

"Good evening, Senator. Dinner will be ready in about half an hour." She smiled at Holly, and Clint said, "This is Miss Moran, Mildred. She'll be staying with us for a few days."

"Pleased to meet you, ma'am." She held the door open for Holly to enter and said, "I've just made some lemonade. Would you like a glass?"

"Yes, that would be nice," Holly said when she stepped into the entrance hall. Clint put his suitcase down and took her arm. "Come into the living room," he said with a smile.

It was a man's room, comfortable, but without the frills a woman might have added. A brown leather sofa was placed at one side of a large stone fireplace, two big matching chairs on the other side. One wall was lined with floor-to-ceiling bookcases that were filled with all manner of books. There were paintings—a Georgia O'Keeffe, a Picasso print of a bullfighter, framed black-and-white sketches of sailing ships and the photograph of a Florida sunset.

A big coffee table held a Remington sculpture, as well as several books and magazines.

"It's a nice room," Holly said, looking around. "You must be comfortable here."

Clint nodded. "I got tired of living in a hotel every time I had to be in Tallahassee, so two years ago I bought the house. I'd like to spend more time here than I do, but it's difficult because of my father. The older he gets the more he depends on me." He shrugged and with a grin said, "He's a difficult man and, believe me, there are times when I'd like to tell him to go to hell, but he's my father. I can't just turn and walk away from him."

"No," Holly said, lowering her gaze. "Of course you can't."

They had dinner in the dining room, a pleasant room with a cedar floor, mahogany table and eight chairs. There were lighted candles on the table. Pink camellias floated in a crystal bowl.

"I figured it was too warm tonight for hot food," Mildred said when she served, first cold gazpacho, then a crabmeat salad. Clint had a glass of white wine; Holly had another glass of lemonade. And they each had two slices of key lime pie.

When they were finished, he said, "Let's have our coffee out on the patio. I don't have much time for gardening, but I like to putter." He took her arm and led her toward the back of the house and out through sliding glass doors.

It was pleasant out here. There were roses, blue gentians and yellow daisies, a camellia tree and a gardenia bush, an orange tree and a grapefruit tree. The garden had a rambly, carefree look that she liked and she smiled thinking of Clint here trimming his roses.

He pulled a wicker chair out from a lawn table, and when they were seated Mildred brought out a tray with their coffee.

"It's nice here," Holly said. "I like your house."

Clint reached for her hand. "Tired?" he asked.

"A little, but it's a nice tired."

"We'll go up as soon as we finish our coffee." He smiled. "Mildred put your things in one of the guest rooms."

"Oh?"

"That doesn't mean you have to stay there."

It was Holly's turn to smile.

"I'm crazy about you, lady." He squeezed her hand. "As soon as Mildred leaves I'm going to carry you upstairs and show you just how crazy." He hesitated and in a more serious tone said, "You don't know how many times I've dreamed of having you here, Holly. In my home, sitting out here with you in the evening."

"I'm going to leave now, Senator," Mildred called from the kitchen. "Do you want anything before I go?"

"No, Mildred. You go ahead. I'll see you in the morning."

They heard the back door close. Clint smiled and, taking Holly's hands, brought her up beside him. "Now, then," he said, "where was I?"

"I believe you mentioned something about showing me the upstairs."

"Ah, yes." He kissed her. "I believe I did."

The bedroom, twice as large as her room at Aunt Lou's, was carpeted in light beige. The drapes, in a heavy homespun fabric, were the same color. A Gauguin print hung on one wall, the portrait of a cowboy on another. There were dark wooden chests with brass handles, a double dresser in the same dark wood. And a bouquet of red roses on the dresser.

Holly looked at Clint. "For me?" she asked.

"To welcome you to my home." He smiled. "There's a saying in Mexico, *mi casa es su casa,* my house is your house." He put his arms around her. "This is your home, Holly."

She rested her head against his shoulder. Her home, she thought. Here with him. How she wished that were true. Clint, her heart cried, I want you so much. I want to live with you, love with you. I want to always be here for you. If it weren't for your father... No! she told herself. Don't think about Jonah tonight. Enjoy the here and now with Clint. Tomorrow will come soon enough.

She stepped out of Clint's arms and moved toward the bed at the far end of the room. It was covered with an old-fashioned hand-crocheted lace spread that seemed oddly out of place in this masculine room.

"How beautiful!" Holly ran her fingers over it. "It's all handmade. It must have taken months for somebody to do this."

"My mother," Clint said. "She was in bed most of the time after Alan was born. This is what she did. I brought very little from the Braxton Beach house, but I wanted this."

"What was she like, Clint?" Holly fingered the delicate lace. "You were so young when she died. Do you remember her?"

"Yes," he said. "I remember. Maybe not so much of what she looked like, but I remember how gentle she was. I remember the smell of her hair and how delicate her arms were when she held me. I remember the day she died."

"Darling," Holly said, and getting up from the bed went to him.

"My father wasn't home. I was alone with her. She held my hand and said, 'Take care of Alan,' and then she... she just went to sleep."

He rarely spoke of his mother to anyone, and when he did, when someone asked, he usually said, "I was very young when she died," and immediately changed the subject. It wasn't that he didn't want to think about his mother, it was more that he didn't want to share his memory of her with anyone. But he had shared it with Holly. That gave him pause and so he turned away and said, "It's late, you need to rest."

She wanted to say, talk about this if you want to, Clint. Tell me about your mother, tell me how painful, how hard, her death was for you. But because he had turned away, she said, "Yes, I'm tired. Do you mind if I take a bath?"

"Of course not. I'll run the water for you."

When he went into the bathroom she unpacked her bag and took out her nightgown and put it on. Clint called out, "Ready," and she went into the bathroom.

It was tiled in dark blue and cream. And in the center of the room, surrounded by leafy green plants, was the biggest bathtub-Jacuzzi she had ever seen. Water, turned dark blue by the color of the tub, swirled with scented bubbles.

She said, "My word!" and when he laughed some of the tension eased.

He kissed the tip of her nose. "Enjoy," he said, and left her alone.

She took her robe and gown off and stepped down into the tub. When she leaned back against a soft blue towel the water covered her breasts. Music, something soft and classical, drifted into the room. She closed her eyes and drifted with it. This was wonderful, soothing, dreamy. If she lived here she'd spend all of her time in the bathroom.

A few minutes later, half-asleep, she heard the door open.

"Mind if I join you?" Clint asked, and without waiting for a reply stepped into the swirling water. He, too, leaned back and closed his eyes. "My favorite room in the house," he murmured.

She kept her eyes closed and listened to the music. In a little while, lulled by the warm water and the music, she relaxed.

"Nice," Clint said.

"Um."

He moved and, lifting her forward and away from the back of the tub, eased in behind her. "I want to hold you like this," he said, and kissed the back of her neck.

With a sigh Holly lay back against him. For a little while he only held her, then he took a bar of soap from the side of the tub and began to soap her breasts and her belly.

"So soft," he whispered. "So nice."

Warmth enveloped her. She closed her eyes and gave herself up to the hands so gently caressing her, to the lips that kissed the back of her neck and her shoulders. And murmured in complaint when he let her go so that he could come around to face her.

"I like to see your eyes go sleepy sexy when I touch you this way," he murmured as he circled around her nipples, drawing ever closer to the tender peaks.

She looked at him, her eyes as green as the sea and filled with love. "Do you know how you make me feel when you touch me like this?" she said.

"I know." He encircled the back of her neck and, drawing her closer, he kissed her mouth. And when he did, when his tongue touched hers, he felt himself grow and knew that soon, oh, yes, soon, they would make love.

She gave herself up to the wonderful things his hands were doing and let herself drift, eyes closed, in a somnolent state of arousal. But in a little while, because she had to touch him, she took the soap and began to wash his chest, making curlicues with his chest hair, then going lower, rubbing the soap across his stomach. And felt her excitement grow.

He leaned back a little, watching her with veiled eyes, scarcely daring to breathe when she took him in her hand.

He gasped and closed his eyes. "Holly," he whispered. "Oh, Holly."

"Do you like it when I touch you this way?" she asked in a voice gone husky with all she was feeling. "Do you want me to stop?"

"No. Lord, no!" But suddenly it was too much; he knew he couldn't wait. With a low cry of need he pulled her closer. With his mouth on hers he grasped her hips, and before she could move or speak he thrust himself inside her, throbbing, swollen with passion he'd barely managed to keep in check.

In a frenzy of desire he caressed her soapy breasts, circling, circling, lightly pinching the erect nipples. When he took her mouth and she answered his kiss, he knew she was as excited as he was.

She moved against him as he moved against her, holding him as he held her, not caring that the water splashed up over the sides of the tub. It didn't matter, nothing mattered except loving. This exquisite loving.

He kissed her mouth and when it began to happen for her, he said, "Tell me, sweetheart. Tell me when."

Instead, caught in the throes of passion, she whispered, "I love you! I love you!"

And as they soared together, he said, "My dearest. My dearest Holly."

Only that.

Three days later they left for Nassau in the Bahamas. Clint had rented a bungalow that was part of a hotel complex, but separate and apart from the hotel as well as from the other cottages and bungalows. It came with a maid whose name was Alice, who arrived every morning to prepare their breakfast. A wonderful breakfast of all kinds of tropical fruit—guavas, soursop, orange papayas and juice-dripping mangoes—ham and eggs and good strong coffee.

In the evening, if they wanted her to and if they were not going out, Alice cooked their dinner.

The first few days she prepared standard United States fare—steak and baked potatoes, lamb chops or a roast of beef. But when Holly asked about typical island food, Alice began serving things like pigeon peas and rice, conch chowder, green turtle pie and baked plantain.

The bungalow, only a hundred yards from the beach, was surrounded by palm trees and tropical flowers of every variety and hue. It was a paradise, lush and luxurious, a perfect place for lovers. Here there were no demands, no pressures. Holly slept well and when at last she arose, Clint rang for Alice, and while she prepared breakfast they went for a morning swim.

The weather was perfect, and although there was talk that a tropical storm was building somewhere off Martinique, here in Nassau the sun shone every day.

One day they rented a car and drove around the island. Another day they strolled through the town. In the waterfront market he bought her a seashell necklace, a floppy straw hat and a multicolored straw bag to go with it.

They swam in the morning to cool off, and at night because it was romantic. Moonlight streaked the water with silver and the waves crested with a phosphorescent light. They usually swam parallel to the shore and when they were tired they floated, rocked by the water as they gazed up at a sky full of stars.

Here, drifting on the water, with the moon shining down, Holly could almost forget what had happened to her in Braxton Beach, and that soon, too soon, they would have to go back.

One night when the waves lifted and brought them closer, Clint wound his legs around hers. She put her arms around his neck and they drifted there in the moonlit water. He eased the straps of her swimsuit down over her shoulders, down to her waist so that he could cup her breasts with his warm, wet hands. With their arms wrapped around each other they sank beneath the surface, mouths clinging, tongues touching, lost in the undersea paradise, soothed by the warm water, cooled by the trade winds when they surfaced.

When they reached the shore Clint picked her up in his arms. He kissed her again, a long, lingering kiss, then hurried with her toward their bungalow.

In their bedroom, he stripped the suit off her, then peeled out of his trunks. He put his arms around her and brought her naked body to his and held her close.

Her skin was cool and smooth as satin. It tasted of the sea. He kissed her and when her body warmed and yearned toward his, he picked her up and laid her on their bed. She clung to him, answering his kiss, and when again, as he had in the water, he cupped her breasts, she sighed and whispered, "Take me Clint. Take me now."

A cry escaped his lips because she wanted him. "Oh, love. Holly, love," he said, and joined his body to hers.

She was all warmth, all giving. He rained kisses over her face, loving this, loving her small cries of passion, her murmured endearments. With each thrust she lifted her body to his, whispering, "More. Oh, please more."

He had never felt so much, and could not help himself when he groaned aloud, when he moved so frantically against her. He who prided himself on his self-control was out of control, reaching, reaching for that one indescribable moment.

"Oh, Clint," she whispered. And the sound of her voice sent him reeling over the edge. It was like sky-rockets going off in his body, like stars breaking into thousands of slivered fragments.

He sought her mouth; he kissed so gently it brought tears to her eyes, kissed the tears away and held her, held her until, exhausted, their bodies still joined, they slept.

* * *

That became the pattern of their days. They ate, they slept and they made love. Each night when the sky was dark they wrapped the soft, thick towels around themselves and went down the beach to the water. When they made sure they were alone they dropped the towels and ran into the surf.

Holly had never swam nude before. She loved it, loved the feel of the warm, velvety water against her skin. And of him, all salt-slick against her, holding her while the water moved against them, his mouth pressed to hers, his hands cupped around her bottom when he entered her. Swaying together when the waves moved against them.

There was something so primitive, so free, about making love this way. Never before had she felt this closeness, this sense of belonging.

They couldn't get enough of each other. They made love most of the night and part of the day. They ate when they were hungry and slept when they were sleepy. One night they dressed and went to one of the restaurants in the hotel. They ordered an expensive meal, but halfway through dinner Clint rested his hand on her thigh. Holly looked at him and it began again.

"This is madness," he said.

"I know."

He signaled for the check, signed it and, taking Holly's hand, led her away from the restaurant. Outside, in the shadowed darkness, he drew her close and kissed her with fevered lips. "I don't know what's happening to me," he said. "You're all I think about. All I want."

They hurried toward their bungalow. He unlocked the door and when they were inside he pulled her down to the floor. It was fast. And good. So unbelievably good.

When it was over they showered together, able to laugh about it now. But soon the laughter died and it began again. Madness, he told himself. Later he said, "You're going to make an old man of me."

She smiled up at him. "Are you complaining?"

"Hell, no!" He kissed her, and his expression changed, became serious. "I never knew anything could be like this, like the way it is between us."

She smoothed the dark hair back from his forehead. "Neither did I," she said.

"I don't want to go back. I want to stay here with you forever, Holly. I never want to stop making love with you."

"Nor I with you," she said.

They lay in each other's arms, and as Holly drifted to sleep a wave of sadness came over her. For though Clint had said he loved making love with her, no word of where this was going had been spoken.

She loved him. She couldn't imagine living the rest of her life without him. But did he love her? Did he feel the same way she did or did the fact that she had been married to his brother still trouble him? When they were making love did he sometimes think that she had once been like this with Alan? Could he ever put that part of her life behind him? Could he ever allow himself to love her?

There had been no communication from Florida. She had phoned both her father and Aunt Lou to let them know where she and Clint were. She didn't know whether or not he had been in touch with his father, but she assumed that he had.

Ever since their arrival in Nassau they'd said almost nothing about Holly's arrest, or that an investigation into the sheriff's office was under way. Now, lying beside him, Holly wondered how far the investigation would go. Would his father be involved, and if he was what would it do to her and Clint's relationship?

She had not told him of her suspicion that it was his father who had been responsible for her arrest. But if she did, when she did . . .

No, she told herself, she wouldn't think about that now.

She snuggled close to Clint. He wrapped his arm around her waist and murmured against her hair. And at last she fell into a troubled sleep.

Chapter Fourteen

The phone rang the next morning when they were having breakfast. Clint answered, said a few words, then, looking concerned, handed the phone to Holly. "It's your father," he said. "He sounds upset."

She took the phone. "Hi, Dad. What's happening?"

"All hell is breaking loose."

"What do you mean?"

"The story broke. It's in all the papers this morning."

"What story, Dad? What are you talking about."

"Sheriff Teasdale has been taken into custody and so has Judge Smith. Your picture is on the front page with that interview you gave the woman attorney from Tallahassee. Lou's phone won't stop ringing and neither will mine here at the Dirty Shame."

For a moment Holly couldn't say anything. Her heart started a tom-tom beat in her chest; her mouth went dry.

She looked at Clint, then quickly away. This was what she had feared. It had started. There would be an investigation. Sheriff Teasdale, for all his bluster and bullying, would probably buckle under questioning. He'd implicate Clint's father. And Clint, because he was Jonah's son, would be hurt, emotionally as well as politically.

With all her heart she wished now that none of this had happened, wished that her father hadn't called the attorney general's office in Tallahassee, and that she hadn't spoken to Jane Bueller. But she had. The wheels of justice were in motion; it was too late to stop them.

She turned to Clint. "The sheriff has been arrested," she said. "Along with Judge Smith."

"Good!"

"That's not all." She heard the hesitation in her father's voice. "Teasdale's sayin' it was Mr. Van Arsdale who put him up to arrestin' you."

Oh, God, she thought. Oh, no.

"There's a picture of him—Jonah—alongside the one of you. And a headline—Senator's Father Implicated In Braxton Beach Scandal."

She felt a wave of dizziness and grabbed the back of a chair for support; this was worse than she had imagined.

"What's the matter?" Clint put his arm around her. "Is it bad? Has something happened to Miss Lou?"

"No," Holly managed to choke out. "No, it...it's not that. I...I think you'd better speak to my father."

He looked puzzled when he took the phone from her. "Yes?" he asked. "What is it, Mr. Moran?"

He listened. His face went white. He clenched his fist. "That's a lie! My father wouldn't..." He shot Holly an agonized look, a look of utter disbelief. "How can they say that?" he said into the phone. "It isn't true. I don't believe it." He listened another moment, said, "Yes, I see. I appreciate your calling, Mr. Moran. I'll make arrangements to fly back to Florida today." He handed the phone to Holly. His expression was tense, unreadable.

She looked at him uncertainly before she took the phone. She spoke for only a minute or two more, and when she hung up Clint said, "I've got to make a call."

To his father. "Yes, of course," she managed to say. "I'll be out on the patio."

He didn't answer. She went out through the sliding glass doors and stood looking out at the water. The day was sunny and bright, the sea an endless turquoise. It hadn't been turquoise last night, it had been velvet black, smooth as silk against their naked bodies when they swam. The waves that brought them together had been touched by moonlight and they had kissed, wet, salt-slick kisses, and she had felt so close to Clint, so much a part of him.

Moonlight slanted across the planes of his face and she had touched him, running her fingers across the broad forehead, his nose, his mouth. He had touched her, too, and the feel of his hands, cool and wet on her skin, made her moan with pleasure.

With his hands around her waist he had raised her above his head, then he brought her slowly down so that their bodies slid against each other. And they had kissed, there in the moonlit sea.

It had seemed to her as though her life, her very being, had begun anew here on this island in the Bahamas. There had been no before, only the here and now, this perfect time with Clint.

It was over. They would leave this tropical island, this dream of happiness they had shared, to return to the real world. To scandal and unwanted publicity. And, if Clint's father really was behind what had happened as she suspected, to the trauma of his father's downfall.

She could hear Clint in the other room. "I'm in Nassau," he said. "I'm flying back to Braxton Beach today. I've just learned that there's speculation about my father being involved in our local scandal. Is that true?"

He listened. "I see," he said in a cold, hard voice. "Yes, I'm sure there's been some mistake. Please tell the governor I'll be in touch with him."

He hung up and made another call. She heard him say, "Dad?" Her stomach tightened; she felt physically sick.

"We'll straighten this out," Clint went on. "Teasdale's trying to find an out for what he did, somebody to blame for his actions. I'll be home today. We'll take care of it."

Jonah would be raving mad. He would blame her, say terrible things to Clint about her.

He put the phone down and saw her standing in the doorway. "You'd better pack," he said.

She hesitated a moment, then turned and started in through the glass doors. He swung around and looked at her. "They're blaming my father for what happened to you," he said.

"I'm sorry." Her voice sounded strangled, tense.

"It's a mistake. I know he has his faults, but he would never..." His face was tortured, his expression unbelieving. "He's my father. He knows how I feel about you. He wouldn't..." His eyebrows drew together in a frown. "You're not saying anything."

She bit her bottom lip and looked away from him.

He took a step toward her. "My God," he said, "you don't think, you can't think, my father was responsible, that he arranged your arrest."

"I don't know," she said so softly he could barely hear. "Somebody...somebody was behind it. Somebody set it up with Buford and Buck and with the sheriff and the judge." She started toward Clint, then stopped. "Somebody with influence," she said. "Somebody like your father."

He stared at her for a moment. She met his gaze and he knew, he saw it in her eyes. She believed his father had arranged her arrest.

"I'm sorry, Clint." She crossed the room and, resting a hand on his arm, said, "I'm so sorry."

He shrugged her hand away and his face was set and angry. "My father has his faults," he said in a voice so deadly cold it sent a shiver of dread down her spine, "but he wouldn't do that. How can you even think he was involved in what happened to you?"

"It was all arranged," she said. "As soon as Buford saw me he made a phone call. When I left the drugstore he left with me. Buck was waiting for us and a few minutes later the sheriff arrived. It had all been planned ahead of time, Clint. Don't you see that?"

"Then somebody else is responsible."

For a moment she didn't respond, then a sigh quivered through her and again she said, "I'm sorry." And knew that it was over between them. That they'd had all they were ever going to have.

"I'll arrange for a plane." He turned away. "You'd better pack."

She wanted to put her arms around him and take away his pain. She said, "Clint?" His shoulders stiffened, but he didn't respond. She waited, then without a word she turned and went into the bedroom.

They had little to say to each other on the flight back to Orlando. There was so much Holly wanted to say, so little she could say. Clint wasn't responsible for his father's actions, yet she knew that when the truth came out it would hurt him as much as it would hurt Jonah. She had not the slightest doubt that he would stand by his father.

When they arrived in Orlando they picked up Clint's car and drove back to Braxton Beach. He took her to her aunt's and carried her luggage to the door. "I'll call you tonight," he said, and started back down the steps.

"Clint…" She searched for the words to tell him how sorry she was about this. But there really weren't any words. Only, "I'm sorry."

"No," he said. "Don't be sorry. None of this is your fault. An injustice was done to you and someone should be punished. But not my father, Holly. You're wrong about him, he couldn't have done this."

He wanted to touch her, to hold her in his arms and pretend that none of this had happened. She was his love. The days they shared together in Nassau had been the happiest of his life. It tightened his gut to know what she had suffered at the hands of the sheriff. She was right when she said someone had to be behind it. Someone, but please, God, not his father. He didn't think he could stand knowing his father had hurt her.

He reached out to touch her hair. He thought of the way it had splayed across his chest when they made love. He remembered midnight swims and the feel of her body close to his when a wave brought them together. His pain was a physical pain deep inside him because he didn't want to leave her. Not this way. Not after what they had shared.

But he did, with a lingering touch, a murmured, "Goodbye, my dear."

When he started the car he looked back and saw her standing there, motionless, as she watched him drive away.

A servant told him his father was in his study. He hurried there, knocked lightly, and when there was no answer he went in. Jonah was standing by the window, looking out at the land that had been in their family for almost a hundred and fifty years. Pine and palms, rolling green lawns and orange groves, acres and acres of groves for as far as you could see.

He said, "Dad?" and his father turned.

"Clint," Jonah said, acknowledging him before he turned back to the window. Almost as though he was speaking to himself, he said, "My granddaddy bought this here land for pennies an acre. Some people said he stole it from the Seminoles. Didn't matter a tinker's damn to the old man what they said. He told me when I was a boy that if you had enough land and enough money words could roll right off your back like water off a gator."

"We need to talk about what's happening," Clint said.

But Jonah went on as though he hadn't heard him. "My daddy, United States Senator Clinton Van Arsdale, was the best wheeler-dealer of 'em all. He bought more land during the depression in the thirties, bought if off of poor dirt farmers who were so desperate they took whatever he offered. In no time at all he had groves all the way from Wauchula on over to Sebring, Indian River and damn near everything in between.''

The old man turned to face Clint. "I followed right along in his footsteps. Bought land, stole land and worked it with migrants. Paid 'em fifty cents a day and charged 'em a dollar a week to sleep in Quonset huts I bought from the government after the war."

He walked over to his desk and poured himself half a glass of brandy. "That was before you and Alan were born," he said. "Once the two of you grew up things changed. You started telling me the migrants deserved better pay and Alan commenced visiting them in the Quonset huts and complainin' to me that I wasn't treatin' them right." He downed half of the glass. "Well, hell, you were my boys so I loosened up, even though it went against my grain."

"You still made plenty of money," Clint said.

"Yeah, I did."

"I'm sorry about the trouble, Dad. We'll work it out, don't worry."

Jonah went to his desk and picked up that morning's newspaper. "You see this?" he asked, and handed it to Clint.

Holly stared up at him. Next to her picture was one of his father. And underneath the caption: Grower Accused Of Controlling Braxton Beach Sheriff And Judge. The story that followed told of Holly's arrest, and of being sentenced to thirty days at the county prison farm by Judge Elmer P. Smith.

"Only a call made by Senator Clint Van Arsdale to the governor's office prevented Miss Moran from being taken directly to the prison farm," the story went on. That was followed by speculation as to why the senator had interfered. The inference was that if his father was indeed responsible for Miss Moran's arrest, then wasn't it strange that the senator had stepped in to free her.

On the following page were photos of Buford and Buck Willaford, with a story outlining their part in what had happened. Willaford declared he was just doing a favor for his friend, Buford Buckaloo. "We were just funnin'," he declared. "Didn't mean Holly no harm."

Buford had at first refused to make a statement. When questioned by someone from the attorney general's office he said he had been advised by his attorney not to say anything.

Clint, sickened by what he had read, threw the paper down on a chair.

"Hell of a mess," his father said. "All because of that damn woman. If she hadn't come back to Braxton Beach none of this would have happened."

"You can't blame Holly for this, Dad. She was the victim, not the perpetrator." Clint looked at his father, his gaze level. "I have to know," he said. "Did you do it? Did you set this whole thing up with Buford, with the sheriff and Judge Smith?"

He waited. It seemed to him as he stood there looking at his father as if everything stopped. He could hear the ticking of the Seth Thomas clock, the whir of the lawn mower from somewhere outside. Don't let it be true, a voice inside his head pleaded. Please, don't let it be true.

"She shouldn't have come back," Jonah said. "She don't belong here, not after what she did. First she ran off with Alan, then she came back and turned her sights on you. I was damned if I was going to stand for it."

He took a hefty pull on the brandy. "Hell, boy, all I wanted to do was shake her up a little, scare her bad enough so she'd get the hell out of Braxton Beach and leave you alone."

Clint stared at his father. The truth hollowed him; it left him chilled and cold as death. For a long time now he had known Jonah had his faults, that he made deals and manipulated men less powerful than himself. But these were small indiscretions, he had told himself. His father had never really hurt anyone before.

"You were getting too interested in her," Jonah said. "I wasn't going to stand by and not do something about it." He gulped down the rest of the brandy. "Maybe...maybe I made a mistake, but if I did it was because I was thinking of your best interests."

"My best interests?"

"That's right. The Moran woman's no good for you." He stepped closer to Clint. "Doesn't it bother you that she was married to your brother? That she slept with him?"

"That's enough, Jonah!"

"Not near enough, but all right." He picked up the bottle and poured another splash into his glass. "Hell, this whole thing'll probably blow over in a day or two. They'll get rid of Teasdale and the judge and maybe slap Buford and Buck on their wrists and that'll be the end of it. But if it's not I'll need a lawyer." He stared down at the liquor. "I'll want you to represent me, of course, but it doesn't need to go that far. You're a senator, you've got influence. Talk to the attorney general. Stop this thing before it goes any further."

"I can't do that."

"Of course you can. Hell, you're a senator, a friend of the governor's." Jonah took a handkerchief out of his pocket and mopped his face. "You're my son, Clint," he said. "It's your bounden duty to help me."

For a long moment Clint didn't answer. He felt a gut-deep sadness, the sadness that comes from knowing something has ended. "All right, Jonah," he said, his voice devoid of emotion. "I'll represent you."

"Thank you, son. I knew you wouldn't desert me."

"But when this is over," Clint went on as though he hadn't heard, "I'll go my way, you go yours."

The color drained from Jonah's face. "What... what're you talking about?"

"I'm going to move to Tallahassee. Permanently. You can get somebody to oversee the groves. Sanchez is a good man. Pay him the right kind of money and he'll work out fine."

"You...you can't leave me!" Jonah's face flushed, his eyes narrowed with anger. "It's because of her," he said. "You're letting her come between us. I told you before and I'll tell you again, she's nothing but a—"

"Stop it!" Clint took a step toward his father, fist clenched, arm raised to strike. The two men stared at each other. Then Clint, without a word, turned and left the room.

Chapter Fifteen

The telephone at Aunt Lou's didn't stop ringing. Either Rosie or Pat, when they were there, fielded the calls. "No," they said over and over again. "Miss Moran has no comment. No, she is not available for an interview."

Reporters gathered on Aunt Lou's front lawn. They rang the doorbell and took pictures through the windows until Rosie pulled down all the shades. They went to the Dirty Shame to try to talk to Pat. He chased them away.

A Miami television station interviewed Phoebe Buckaloo. She declared her son's innocence. "Buford's a good boy," she said. "It's that Moran woman who's causing all this trouble."

If this was difficult for Holly she knew how devastating it must be for Clint. How torn he must be between loyalty to his father and what he felt for her.

Their time together in Nassau now seemed like a distant dream. She loved Clint with all her heart, but was love enough? They might have been able to put aside the memory of her marriage to Alan, but this with his father would always stand between them. What Jonah had done was spiteful and vicious; she would never forgive him.

She made her decision—as soon as she could she would leave Braxton Beach.

"Don't go," her father said that night when she told him. "This is your home. Stay here with us."

She shook her head and as gently as she could said, "Braxton Beach hasn't been my home for a long time, Dad. I have a job in New Orleans, a home and friends. That's where I belong, not here."

No, not here in this old-fashioned house on a quiet tree-lined street. Not here in this cozy kitchen where they were now, the four of them, her father, her aunt and Rosie O'Toole.

There were so many memories here, memories of Aunt Lou bustling around the kitchen, stirring oatmeal while Holly set the table. Aunt Lou asking if she'd done her homework, turning to smile, making sure Holly drank her milk.

Other memories. Of the morning Clint had held her in the rocking chair. And the morning when, after a night of love, they sat at this same table holding hands and touching.

"If there's a trial you'll have to be here," Rosie said.

"I'll come back when I'm needed."

"You'll stay until everything is over?" Aunt Lou asked.

"I guess that depends on how long it will all take."

"What about Clint?" Pat wanted to know. "Where does he stand in all this?"

"It must be real hard on him," Aunt Lou said. "His father on one side of the fence, you on the other."

"Yes, I'm sure it is."

Pat took a sip of his coffee. "You know how I feel about the Van Arsdales, but Clint's different. He's not like Alan and he's not like his father."

"I know that, Dad." Holly twisted her cup back and forth on the saucer and tried to blink back tears. "I care for Clint," she said, "but I'm afraid there's too much in the past for us ever to have a future together."

Aunt Lou took her hand. "Maybe things will work out if you stay, dear."

"No," Holly said. "I can't. As soon as this is over I'm going back to New Orleans."

There was nothing they could say to dissuade her.

Holly was still in bed the next morning when Clint called. "I'd like to see you," he said. "Will you have dinner with me tonight?"

She sat up and smoothed the tumbled hair back from her face. "Yes, Clint, of course."

"I'll pick you up at six. I thought we'd drive out to the restaurant on the beach we went to that day after church."

"I'd like that."

"Are you all right?"

She held the phone against her cheek for a moment before she said, "Yes, Clint, I'm fine. And you?"

"A little rough around the edges."

She heard the tension in his voice and said, "I'll see you tonight, Clint. Take care." When she hung up she lay back against the pillows thinking about him, about how hard this must be for him. And wondering why he wanted to see her. Was he going to tell her that because of his father it would be best not to see her again?

She washed her hair, something she always did in a moment of crisis. She took a bubble bath, polished her nails and gave herself a pedicure. That night she tried on three different outfits before she decided on the same pale green silk she'd worn the first time she had dinner with him.

She put her makeup on, dabbed perfume behind her ears. At five-thirty she was ready. And as nervous as though this was a first date.

When she went downstairs she pulled a curtain back, peeked out of the window and said a silent prayer of thanks that no reporters were camped outside.

Clint greeted her almost formally when he arrived. He said hello to her aunt and gave Lou a box of chocolates. He said, "Are you ready, Holly?" and when she said that she was he opened the door for her to precede him out to his car. He didn't take her arm or attempt to touch her.

The evening was as pleasant as only a late summer's evening in Florida can be. When they reached the beach road, Clint, after asking if Holly minded, switched off the air-conditioning and let the windows down.

The sun set in a blaze of flamingo red and the sky slowly changed to pink, then to mauve with streaks of light that filtered through the blue-gray of the coming night. One by one the stars appeared and a crescent moon rose over the water.

He put a tape on and turned it low so they could talk. But they said little, other than to remark on the sunset, or how calm the Gulf seemed at this time of evening.

"The calm before the storm," Clint said. "That tropical depression near Martinique has turned into a full-blown hurricane named Betsy. If it keeps going in that direction it will probably hit Haiti and mainland Cuba."

"If it does do you think it will hit the Florida coast?"

"It's too early to tell, but I hope not. We've just started picking. A storm like Betsy could wipe out this year's crop." He turned to look at her for a moment and said, "But that's really no concern of mine. I no longer have any interest in the orange groves. I'll supervise this year's picking, but as soon as it's in that's it. I'm leaving Braxton Beach. Tallahassee will be my permanent home."

"You're . . . you're leaving your home here?"

"My father's house," he said dryly. "It hasn't been a home for a long time, not since my mother died, not since Alan left." He speeded up to pass a car. "I stayed on because Jonah asked me to take charge of the groves. I like the work and I liked working with the men, but it's time to leave. I've had a standing offer to join a prestigious law firm in Tallahassee, but I think maybe I'd rather open my own office there."

"I see." But she didn't, not really. Was Clint leaving because of his father or because of her? She looked out at the darkening night. "I'll be leaving soon, too," she said. "I'm going back to New Orleans."

The car swerved. But when he spoke his voice showed no emotion. "When?" he asked.

"As soon as this . . . this business about the sheriff has been settled. If it goes to trial I may have to testify."

His face tightened. "Yes," he said. "I suppose you will." He waited, trying to frame the words, and finally said, "My father has asked me to represent him."

"And you're going to."

"He's my father."

"I see."

They spoke little after that. When they arrived at the restaurant they were shown to a table on the terrace overlooking the water. He ordered a bourbon and soda; Holly asked for Perrier with a twist of lime.

She looked lovely tonight, he thought. The green dress matched her eyes; her hair was a soft dark cloud about her face. At seventeen she had been pretty, a little uncertain, a little awkward. Now, some ten years later, she had grown into a poised and beautiful woman. A desirable woman.

He thought then, as he sometimes did, of that long-ago day when she had fallen into his arms from the orange tree. He remembered the scent of oranges and the musky smell of her skin. They lay there together under the orange tree, arms and legs entangled, the ripe fruit scattered all around them and he had thought, If I kiss her now she'll kiss me back. But he hadn't kissed her, because she was Alan's girl.

How different it all might have been if she'd been his girl instead of Alan's. In spite of the fact that she was only seventeen he would have wooed her and won her. He would have taught her the many ways of love. And loved her. Oh, yes, he would have loved her.

Ten years. They would have had children. But those years and the children that might have been were lost to him because she married Alan. Was it too late for them? With all that had happened, with all that stood between them, did they have any hope of a future together?

They ordered, but only picked at their food. Holly was silent, withdrawn. Once he said, "You look great with a tan," then wished he hadn't because the tan reminded him of Nassau.

Sometimes, after Alice the maid had cleared up their breakfast dishes and left, he and Holly would sun on the patio. The first time he said, "You're going to have a white line in the back where your bathing suit strap ties. Let me unfasten it for you."

"Only if your intentions are honorable," she'd said.

"Of course they are," he said, pretending outrage. He unfastened the straps. "Oil?" he asked.

"Carefully," she said with a smile in her voice.

He drizzled oil on her skin and began to rub it in. She murmured, "Um," and gave herself up to his hands.

He massaged the oil into her skin, marveling at how perfectly she was put together—nice shoulders, slim waist, long tapering legs. He slid his hands around to her breasts. She said, "Hey, what're you doing?"

"The skin here is tender," he told her. "It might burn."

"Uh-huh," she said. And rolled onto her back. "Can anybody see us?"

"Only the sea gulls."

"Then put some of the oil on my breasts." And when he did, she murmured, "Oh, that's nice. So nice."

His hands were warm; her skin was hot. He said, "I guess you know what you're doing to me?" And she smiled up at him.

He pulled the bottom part of her suit down. He drizzled the hot oil over her stomach and rubbed her there, then the inside of her thighs. She said, "Darling? Darling, please," and like a man on fire he yanked his trunks off. They made love there with the sun beating down on them, slow, hot, oily love. And it was then, then when she looked up at him and said, "Oh, Clint. Oh, darling," that he knew how much he loved her.

He wished now that they had never left Nassau, wished they had stayed forever on that island in the sun where there were no yesterdays, no tomorrows.

They finished dinner. Neither of them wanted dessert. Clint asked for the bill and when he had paid it he said, "I'd like to walk for a while. Do you mind?"

They left the restaurant and went down toward the beach. Holly took her shoes off and left them on the steps. The sand was still warm from the sun of the day and it felt good against her bare feet. The night was quiet, there was no one else on the beach.

"I'm going to miss this," she said.

"When you go back to New Orleans."

"Yes."

"To Jacques Dupre?"

"I told you, there's nothing between us but friendship, a friendship that's important to me."

"I see." He put his hands on her shoulders and turned her so that she faced him. "I wish there had never been anyone else in our lives," he said. "I wish you had married me instead of Alan. I wish we'd had children together." He tilted her face up and looked in her eyes. "A little girl who looked exactly like you, and a boy with hair as red as Pat Moran's."

She felt as if her heart were breaking. "And another boy," she said in a voice choked by all she was feeling. "A tall, serious boy with gray eyes and a lock of dark hair that fell over his forehead the way yours does."

He put his arms around her and drew her close. "When this is over," he said. "This thing with the sheriff...with my father..." He stopped, his face against her hair. He had said he would defend his father. When he did he would have to put Holly on the stand and ask her questions about her arrest. The whole ugly thing would surface; it would hurt her.

He felt the brush of her hair against his face and breathed in the scent of her. He tilted her face to his and when he saw the tears that rose and fell he kissed her. And in his kiss was all of his sorrow, his pain and his passion. He kissed her eyelids, licked her tears and held her as though he would never let her go.

"Don't cry," he said. "Don't cry."

And when at last he let her go he took her hand and led her back down the beach the way they had come.

Rosie O'Toole arrived at Aunt Lou's the following morning in time for breakfast. She brought a box of hot cinnamon buns from Olson's bakery, along with copies of both the local paper and the *Miami Herald*.

She helped Miss Lou to the kitchen table, started a pot of coffee and, when she saw Holly coming downstairs from her bedroom, said, "Good morning. I brought the papers. I thought you should see them before the phones start ringing again."

Holly tightened the belt of her yellow robe. She kissed her aunt's cheek, then asked, "What is it now? What's happened."

Rosie handed her a copy of the *Miami Herald*. "This," she said.

Holly sat down and opened the paper. The big, black headline glared up at her: Father Of Senator Van Arsdale Questioned In Braxton Beach Case. Indictment Expected.

"It's going to be one hell of a brouhaha, isn't it?" Rosie said.

Holly put the paper down. "I'm afraid so."

"I'm sorry for Clint. Must be hard on him, feeling the way he does about you. Bet old Jonah is raising hell right about now. What he'd better do is get himself a good lawyer."

"He has a good lawyer. He has Clint."

Aunt Lou stared at her. "Clint's going to represent him? But that... that's like taking his father's side against you."

"Jonah is his father," Holly said. "I'm sure he feels a family obligation."

The phone started ringing. Aunt Lou said, "I bet it's those reporter people again."

And Rosie said, "Do you want me to answer it?"

"Please," Holly said.

Reporters gathered outside the house. When Rosie left for the hospital she had to elbow her way through them. The phone kept ringing. For a while Holly answered, but after a few calls, tired of repeating, "No comment," she simply disconnected the phone.

There was nothing she could say. The wheels of justice had started turning. There was nothing she could do.

There were a thousand things to take care of before he went back to Tallahassee. He visited all the groves. He gave his managers and the workers a raise and reassured them that everything would go on as before. Over his father's objections, saying, "I can't help you unless I know everything I can about your business dealings," he went through everything in Jonah's office, his father's files and his father's desk.

Much of what he discovered appalled him—shady land deals, pressure exerted on a man or a company in trouble, the control Jonah had over the office of the sheriff, the finagling he'd done to get Elmer P. Smith appointed to the bench. The money he'd made from the labor of inmates at the county farm.

It was all there, the wheelings and dealings, the contrivances, the dossiers of men he had brought down, the misuse of money and power.

Holly's return to Braxton Beach had been the catalyst for his father's downfall, not the cause. She had been a victim, just as all of the other people his father had hurt over the years had been victims.

He sat in Jonah's chair, head back, eyes closed, empty inside because he knew that whatever love he had felt for his father was dead. The words *honor thy father* echoed in his mind. But he could no longer honor Jonah. The knowledge saddened him as nothing else ever had. He would do what he could to defend Jonah, but when he had it would be over between them.

And Holly? Alan had wronged her; his father had hurt her. If she had any sense she'd get as far away from the Van Arsdale family as she could.

She had so much to forgive. Would she ever be able to? Was the love they felt for each other strong enough to withstand all that had happened?

He went to the window and looked out. It was a gray day; the sky was heavy with threatening clouds.

The time they had spent together seemed like a distant dream of what might have been if things had been different.

"Holly." He said her name into the silence of the room. "Holly. Holly, my love."

His throat knotted with pain, he felt the sting of tears.

That night on the six o'clock news came word that Hurricane Betsy had hit Haiti with winds of more than one hundred and twenty miles an hour. If it didn't weaken over land it would surely hit Cuba. And Florida?

"Too early to tell," the weatherman said. "But this is a dangerous storm, folks. You'd better be prepared."

Chapter Sixteen

The lady named Betsy hit Guantánamo Bay, Cuba, with gusts up to one hundred and forty miles an hour. It tore through Camagüey, then veered off the land and up toward Andros Island. It ripped through the island, blowing roofs off houses, tearing up trees, then headed out to sea where it stalled.

The Hurricane Center in Miami tried to decide if the storm had blown itself out or was gearing up to hit land again. And if it was, where would it hit? A reconnaissance plane was sent out and reported back that Betsy was regaining strength. But there was no indication where she would head next.

In Braxton Beach it rained for two days and two nights, while townspeople waited, not sure whether to go into full hurricane preparation or not.

Farmers were worried and so were the owners of orange groves, like Jonah, who feared they would lose everything if Betsy hit.

Things were bleak enough without the weather turning bad, Holly thought as she gazed out of the window at the slanting rain. Aunt Lou had a cold and didn't want the air-conditioning on. It was summer hot inside the house without it, the air outside, muggy, still, as though waiting for the storm to strike.

And Murph O'Brien, preparing himself for the storm should it come, fortified himself with a pint of Irish and fell down his cellar stairs again. Mrs. O'Brien reported the accident to Pat, saying, "He was singing when the ambulance took him away." This time with a broken hip.

"I hate to ask you, darlin'," Pat said when he called Holly the next afternoon to tell her about Murph. "I can manage all right tonight, but tomorrow's Saturday and the bar will be swamped. Could you come and help me out?"

"If you want me to, of course. But I just heard on the news that the hurricane is gathering force. The weather people are saying it will probably hit the Florida Keys. After that it's anybody's guess whether it will hit the east coast or the west."

"Or cross the Gulf and head for Mexico," Pat said. "If it turns toward us I'll board up, but I'll bet you a nickle it's goin' to head straight for Mexico. Can you come early, like maybe six-thirty to help me start settin' up?"

"Okay," she said.

"If it does decide to come our way we'll have ourselves a hurricane party."

When Holly put the phone down she went into the kitchen where Hattie was preparing lunch. "Can you stay over this weekend?" she asked. "My dad needs me at the Dirty Shame tomorrow night and I don't want to leave Aunt Lou here by herself."

"I'd like to stay." Hattie added another scoop of mayonnaise to the potato salad. "This house is a lot sturdier than mine. If something happens I'd rather be here."

And so it was agreed. Holly would drive Hattie home after lunch so the older lady could make sure her house was closed up tight, and pack a bag with the clothes she would need for the weekend.

As soon as they finished lunch, Holly said, "The rain has stopped, Hattie. I think we'd better go before it starts up again."

They went out to the car. The air was still, sticky with humidity. "The calm before the storm," Holly murmured, remembering Clint's words. And prayed that Betsy wouldn't come this way.

She drove Hattie home, helped her put towels under the doors in case the wind blew the rain in and made sure one window was left open a few inches the way you were supposed to in a hurricane.

When they got back to the house, Lou said, "Clint called. He wants you to call him."

Holly started for the phone, then stopped. What if Jonah answered? She was about to ask Hattie to make the call for her when Aunt Lou said, "He's at the Flamingo Hotel, room 402. He left the number."

The hotel? Puzzled, Holly reached for the phone. The hotel switchboard rang his room. He didn't answer. She put the phone down, puzzled. Why was he at the hotel instead of his home? Had something happened with his father? A rift, because of her?

She tried again later and when his room didn't answer she left another message that she had called. It was after midnight before he called her back.

"I had to go to Wauchula to check on the groves there," he said. "I'm sorry it's so late. How's your aunt? Are you boarding up?"

"Not yet," Holly said. "Do you think we need to?"

"It'd be a good idea. If you'd like I'll send somebody over in the morning to take care of it."

"Yes, that would be great, Clint. I really don't know anybody to call."

"If the storm does veer our way I'd like to stay with you and your aunt. I'm going to have to go to Sebring tomorrow, but I'll be back later. I'll see you tomorrow night."

"I won't be here," she said. "Dad asked me to help him out at the bar. I'm going over about six." She wanted to ask why he was at the hotel instead of his home, instead she said, "Do you think the storm will hit us?"

"That's anybody's guess, Holly. But, yes, I've got a feeling it will. If it turns toward the east coast it won't hurt us too badly, but if it comes up through Naples and Fort Myers we could be in trouble."

"How much damage do you think it will do to the groves?"

"If we get a direct hit it will certainly ruin this year's crop. Actually it could wipe us out for the next couple of years." He hesitated, then said, "But that's not my problem. I moved out last night. I should have done it years ago. I would have, but I thought my father needed me. I know better now. He doesn't need me or anybody else. From now on, as far as I'm concerned, I don't have a father."

"Oh, Clint." She felt so deep-down sorry because if she hadn't come back to Braxton Beach this wouldn't have happened.

"My father was responsible for your arrest," he went on. "I'll never forgive him."

"He's your father, Clint. You can't . . . you can't just turn your back on him."

"I can and I have." He sounded bitter. "He can have the groves. I'm walking away from them and from him." For a moment he didn't say anything. She waited, then he said, "We have a lot to talk about, Holly. I'll come to the Dirty Shame tomorrow night as soon as I get back from Sebring."

"All right, Clint."

"There's so much I want to say to you. But it will wait until tomorrow."

Tomorrow. She held the phone close to her cheek as though to be closer to him. "Tomorrow," she said.

There was a moment of hesitation before he said, in a voice filled with both sadness and passion. "Good night, my love."

My love. She replaced the phone. And for the first time in their relationship felt a soaring hope that perhaps, after all, they might have a chance together.

Betsy was no lady. She devastated Andros Island, then, girding her hurricane winds, swept over the Florida Keys with a force that knocked out bridges and tore up part of Highway 1. Residents, warned in advanced, congregated in schools and churches. Roofs were blown off; newer houses, built less solidly than older ones, collapsed in the one-hundred-and-forty-mile-an-hour wind.

As soon as Holly awoke that morning she turned on her bedside radio. Betsy hovered in the Gulf, the weatherman reported. "It could go either way," he said, "out over the Gulf toward Tampico, Mexico, or up the west coast of Florida. We won't know for several hours, but it's best to prepare. This is one heck of a storm. Take every precaution."

She hurried out of bed, dressed and went down to the kitchen. Hattie had breakfast on the table. "The fellas came a few minutes ago to board up the windows," she said. "Going to be hot as hades in here."

"My cold is better," Aunt Lou said. "I guess we'll have to turn the air-conditioning on."

"And I've got to check the larder," Holly said. "I want to make sure we have extra batteries for the radio and a good supply of candles. We'll want to fill everything that's fillable, even the bathtub, with water."

"I bought candles last year when there was a hurricane warning," Lou said. "It didn't come and probably this won't, either." Indicating the cupboards, she said, "The candles are in the bottom drawer."

As soon as breakfast was over, Holly went into town. She bought the extra batteries for the radio, and even though there was a good supply of candles, bought another half dozen. After that she bought fruit, some canned goods, bread and cheese. If Betsy hit it was best to be prepared. Then, remembering her aunt's prescription, she went to Ungerliter's Drugstore.

"Storm's headed our way," he said. "Just come on the news. Starting on up toward Naples. Keeps coming it'll hit us sometime tonight."

She hurried home and, as soon as she had put her purchases away, called her father at the saloon. "I just heard that the storm is headed our way."

"There's still a chance she'll head out into the Gulf."

"You're not going to open tonight, are you?"

"Why sure I am. Been gettin' calls ever since I got here, people wantin' to know if we'd be open. Some of them said they'd rather be here than anywhere else."

She knew it wasn't a good idea. Although the patrons of the Dirty Shame rarely drank too much, they drank enough to loosen them up. She wasn't sure "loosening up" was a good idea during a hurricane. Ten or twelve years ago the tenants of an apartment building along the Mississippi coastline got together for a hurricane party. They were warned to go to higher ground, but they didn't go. The apartment house went down; there were no survivors.

"All right," Holly said with a sigh. "I'll be there." But even as she put the phone down she felt a niggle of fear. Somehow she knew this wasn't a good idea.

The rain started that afternoon, a heavy pelting rain that seemed a precursor of what was to come. Rosie O'Toole stopped by on her way home from the hospital.

"Pure nonsense," she said when she learned that Pat intended to keep the saloon open and that Holly was going to help him out. "It's not so much that any of the customers will be in danger, the place is strong enough. The problem is that if the storm strikes while they're there they'll all have to stay till it's over. Which means," she said, laughing, "that your dad will do one hell of a business. You'd better plan on being there all night, Holly. If it's all right with you I'll stay here with Miss Lou and Hattie."

"It's more than all right," Holly said gratefully. "I'll feel a lot better knowing you're here."

The rain had stopped by the time she left for her father's place, and the air was so still not even a leaf moved. It gave her an eerie feeling that everything was just poised and waiting. She drove the four miles to the Dirty Shame and parked behind her father's old brown sedan.

There were only a few customers when she went in. Pat gave her a hug and set her to work slicing potatoes for french fries and opening bags of chips. The television over the bar was on and reporting updates on Betsy.

"She's headed straight up the west coast," the newscaster from the Miami bureau reported, "packing winds of one hundred and forty with gusts over one hundred and sixty."

That scared her, not for herself, but for Clint who would be driving back from Sebring. As much as she wanted to see him she hoped he would stop and stay at a motel.

People began drifting into the bar. The Raffertys brought a wicker basket filled with sandwiches. "In case we're here for a while," Molly Rafferty said. A few minutes later Mr. Gomez came in with tortillas and the makings for tacos. By the time Jimmy Collins came to play the piano everybody was in a festive mood, as though preparing for a party instead of a hurricane.

It started raining again about seven-thirty and the customers who came in after that were carrying umbrellas and wearing raincoats. Business was brisk; everybody was cheerful. About ten that night the wind started, gusting at first, then turning into a steady blow that increased by the hour.

The customers looked at one another uneasily, wondering, Holly guessed, if it really had been a good idea to come out tonight. Pat got out the candles for the bar and Holly lighted the table candles, just in case.

Just in case came a few minutes later when, with a strong gust of wind, all the lights went out.

"It makes for a more romantic evening," Pat joked. A few of the customers laughed; the others were silent, worried.

As was Holly, not so much about what would happen to the Dirty Shame or the people here tonight, but about Clint. When the phone rang, sure that it was Clint, she grabbed it.

"Clint there?" a man asked.

She didn't recognize the voice. "No," she said. "I'm expecting him, though. Would you like him to call you back, Mr. . . . ?"

"This . . . this here's his father." He was panting, breathless. "Tell him . . . tell him to call me. Trees're blowing down, all the oranges. . ." His voice faded, grew weaker. "Something hit me, broke my arm, cut my . . . head. Tell Clint. Tell . . ."

"Mr. Van Arsdale," Holly said. "Mr. Van Arsdale . . ." The line went dead. She jiggled the phone; nothing happened.

Pat said, "Who was it?"

"Clint's father."

"Jonah? What did he want."

"He was looking for Clint. He's been hurt." If the phones weren't out of order she could call the police, an ambulance. But the phones weren't working. What if

Jonah was badly hurt? He'd said he'd cut his head. God knows she had no love for the man, but he was Clint's father. Could she stand by and not do anything?

She grabbed her raincoat from the hook behind the bar. Pat said, "Where do you think you're goin'?"

"To the Van Arsdales'," Holly answered as she headed for the door.

"Over my dead body."

"Jonah's hurt, Dad. I can't *not* do something. Clint should be here soon. Tell him where I am." And before Pat could say anything else, she ran out the door. Into the storm.

A gust of wind hit the car and it swerved. Clint tightened his hands on the wheel. He knew he should take the next exit off the road and find a motel. Knew it, but he kept going because he'd promised Holly he would see her tonight. He wanted to be with her; if it meant racing the wind, then so be it.

He knew now that he loved her. Maybe he'd loved her since that long-ago day in the orange grove. It didn't matter that she had been Alan's wife. She and Alan happened a long time ago; that was the past, this was the future. He wanted a life with her, to have children together. They could— A powerful gust of wind hit and, as though slammed by a giant fist, the car careered to the right. Clint held it, swore under his breath and made it back to the center of the road. Nobody else was out tonight; anybody with any sense had found a safe shelter.

He knew he should stop, but he kept going because he had to be with Holly.

He said her name aloud, "Holly," and did not know why he felt such a growing sense of unease.

* * *

The rain blinded her. Like the wind, it came in pelting gusts, shaking the car, making it difficult to keep on the road. It was worse when she left the town and took the narrow road that led to the Van Arsdale groves. She crawled along at twenty miles an hour, and sighed with relief when at last her headlights picked up the sign that said Van Arsdale, Private Property, and turned in.

Clint's father wouldn't be happy to see her. He might not open the door when he discovered who it was. But he was Clint's father and his voice had sounded shaky over the phone. She had no way of knowing whether the phone had simply gone dead, as had all of the others in town, or if he had lost consciousness. If that was the case she had to try to help him.

A mile and ten minutes later she pulled into the driveway. The wind had increased in intensity; she wasn't sure she could make it up the stairs and to the front door without being blown away. And what if Jonah, when he saw who it was, wouldn't let her in? She wasn't sure she could make it back to her father's bar. Nevertheless, she had come this far, she had to try.

With a muttered oath, Holly took a flashlight out of the glove compartment, opened the door and sprinted for the steps. A gust of wind caught her on the top step. She was whirled around and barely managed to save herself by grabbing on to one of the pillars. Then bending low, almost blinded by the rain, she made her way to the door and rapped the big brass knocker.

The house was in darkness. She knocked again, knocked as hard as she could before she tried the door. The knob turned, the door opened and she stepped inside.

"Mr. Van Arsdale?" she said. Then louder, "Mr. Van Arsdale, are you here?"

There was no answer, at least none she could hear above the roar of the wind. She flashed a beam of light around and saw that she was in an entrance hall. She went forward, calling out, "Mr. Van Arsdale? Are you here? Is anybody here?"

Through the living room into another hall. Other rooms opened off of it, and down toward the end of the hall she saw a flicker of light. And again she called out, "Mr. Van Arsdale?"

She went toward the light and into the room. It appeared to be a study, with a desk and executive chair, a fireplace, a few straight-backed chairs and a sofa. The windows and the French doors at one end of the room had been boarded up. There was a lighted candle on the desk.

She shone the light around the room. Jonah Van Arsdale lay half on, half off the sofa. She approached and he said, "Clint? Clint, is that you?"

"No," she said. "It's Holly...Holly Moran, Mr. Van Arsdale."

He managed to raise himself on one elbow. A streak of lightning zinged through the room and she saw the cut on the side of the head, the blood running down his face. "You're hurt," she said.

"Stay away from me." His voice was weak, but filled with venom.

"I want to help you."

"I don't want your help. Where's Clint? Where's my boy?"

"He went to Sebring. He said he'd be back tonight."

"He won't be able to, not in this storm." The house shook; somewhere an unshuttered window broke. "Hell of a blow," Jonah muttered, talking to himself. "Going to ruin the oranges. Have to go out, see what I can save."

He pushed himself up off the sofa, rocked onto his feet, staggered and grabbed the back of a chair.

"You can't go out in this. You're hurt, you—"

"Don't need your help." He turned on her, his eyes narrowed, his face full of hatred. "Stole Alan from me, killed him in that accident. Now you've come back aiming to have Clint." He took an unsteady step toward her. "You won't get him. I'll see you in hell before I let that happen."

He propelled himself toward the fireplace and grabbed an andiron. "Get out of here!" he shouted. "Get out before I . . ." He swayed, reached for the fireplace mantel, steadied himself and reeled toward her, andiron raised, ready to strike.

Holly stood rooted, unable for a moment to move, her mouth dry, heart plunging like a wild bird in her chest, unable to say more than, "Mr. Van Arsdale . . . don't!"

He stared at her. There was blood running down his forehead. A gust of wind slammed against the house, the boards that shuttered the glass doors at the end of the room tore off, and went spinning through the darkness. Glass shattered into the room. Lightning streaked outside and for a moment they could see orange trees, uprooted, bent by the terrible force of the wind that now invaded the room.

"The trees!" Jonah screamed, and headed for the broken-glass doors.

"No, no, you can't go out there. You can't—"

But he was past hearing as he plunged through the broken door outside into the force of the hurricane.

* * *

"Holly isn't here?" Clint stared at Pat. "But she told me this is where she would be."

"It's where she was," Pat snapped. "She left maybe twenty minutes ago."

"In this storm? What in the hell is the matter with you, letting her go out in this?"

"She didn't wait for my approval. Your father called here for you. Said he was hurt. Then the phone went dead and Holly lit out. I been goin' crazy with worry. I—"

But Clint had already turned and run back into the storm.

He drove faster than he should have, but this wasn't the time for caution. Branches hit the car; a hard plastic garbage can banged off the hood. It was all he could do to keep the car on the road. A piece of plywood off somebody's door came sailing down the street straight at him. He swerved just in time.

He couldn't think coherently. Only scattered thoughts. Holly. Oh, God, she was out in this. She'd gone to the house. His father was hurt. He turned off the road onto the private road. With a flash of lightning he saw the devastation, downed trees, uprooted shrubs. He pulled into the driveway and, bending so low he was almost hugging the ground, made it onto the porch and into the house.

"Holly!" he called. "Holly, where are you?"

He ran through the darkened house calling her name, stumbling over furniture, cursing because he didn't have a flashlight. Into the hall leading to the study, feeling his way. Saw the flicker of a light and ran toward it, crying out, "Holly! Holly!"

"Clint?" She stood in the doorway. "Clint, hurry!" she cried. "Your father—"

"What?" He reached her, grabbed her. "Are you all right?"

"Yes, yes. But your father..." She pulled him into the room. "He's outside. He ran outside."

He saw the broken door, and the room, everything blown by the wind, chairs overturned, books scattered. "Get out of here," he ordered. "Stay in the hall where it's safe." He snatched the flashlight out of her hand and started for the broken door.

"No! Don't go out there. You can't!" But the wind took her voice; he didn't hear. She hesitated a moment, then turned and ran after him.

He was out of the door before he saw her. He screamed, "Get back!"

Instead she grabbed his hand.

"Dammit, Holly..." In the flash of lightning he saw her white face, hair plastered to her head by the rain, the determined look. "Get behind me," he said. "Hang on to my belt."

She did as he told her, leaning tight to his body, clutching his belt with both hands. Tree limbs swept past them, and oranges, like a hail of round bullets, blew past. She could see the beam of the flashlight sweeping the ground. Then, under one of the trees, she saw Jonah.

"There he is!" she cried.

Clint ran forward, pulling her with him, and fell to the ground beside his father. Jonah was unconscious. Holly knelt beside him and reached for his pulse. There was a faint, irregular beat. "We've got to get him inside," Clint said.

He grabbed his father's feet. "I'll have to pull him," he shouted above the wind. "He's too big to carry."

"I can help." She took one of Jonah's legs and, together, pulling as hard as they could, almost beaten down by the wind and slashed by the rain, they made their way slowly back to the house. Once they had to stop to rest. Once Holly stumbled and fell. But slowly, oh, so slowly, bodies bent into the wind, they reached the house and dragged Jonah inside.

"We've got to...to get him to the hall," Clint panted. "I can do it. There are more candles in the desk. Get them."

She found three candles, grabbed them, then ran across the room and slammed the door behind her. They lighted the candles and looked down at Jonah. His left arm bent at a crazy angle and blood oozed from the cut on his forehead. Holly took her white blouse off, Clint tore off one of the sleeves and wrapped it around his father's head.

All they could do now was wait for the storm to abate, and hope to God his father didn't die. He reached for Holly and pulled her close.

They sat there, all through that dark and cruel night, keeping their vigil beside his father.

Jonah Van Arsdale died that night without regaining consciousness. Clint held his hand and when Jonah breathed his last Clint said, "He's gone. My father is dead."

Chapter Seventeen

The day after Jonah's funeral the sun came out and the air was as fresh as though after a summer rain. But much had been destroyed by the storm. The Dirty Shame lost part of its roof. Two of the shutters had blown off Aunt Lou's, resulting in broken windows and soaked carpets. Some of the stores along the main street, like Mr. Ungerliter's drugstore, had been badly damaged.

But it was the farmers and the orange growers who suffered the most from Hurricane Betsy.

The Van Arsdale groves lay in ruin.

"Is it all gone?" Holly asked when she stood in the doorway of the Van Arsdale house with Clint, looking out at what was left of the thousands of trees that only a few days ago had been filled with oranges ready for picking.

"With luck and hard work it will come back in two or three years, but for now..." He shook his head, then took her hand and together they went outside and walked through the storm-ravaged groves. Only a few trees were left standing, the rest had been uprooted, torn from the earth as though by a giant hand. Oranges were scattered all around them. He picked one up, then held it to his nose and sniffed.

"The scent of oranges," he said. "Do you remember?"

"Yes, I remember."

"You were as young as springtime, as beautiful as any girl I'd ever seen."

"You frightened me and I fell into your arms."

"And I fell in love." He touched her face. "I'm still in love, Holly. So much in love it hollows me inside." He gathered her in his arms; he kissed her and against her lips he whispered, "Will you marry me? Will you live with me and be my love for always and forever?"

She touched her lips to his. "Yes," she said. "Oh, darling, yes."

On the first day of October Holly walked down the aisle of the Braxton Beach Community Church on her father's arm. She wore a pale pink gown and carried a bouquet of pink camellias.

When they reached the altar her father kissed her cheek, then placed her hand in Clint's before he stepped back. She looked up at Clint. She saw the love in his eyes, the promise of their future.

Rose Varnum sang "Oh, Perfect Love" and when she finished the Reverend Richardson opened his Bible.

"Dearly beloved," he began.

Late-afternoon sun filtered through the stained-glass windows. From outside Holly heard the trill of a bird.

She felt a sense of unreality that she was here in this place. With Clint.

Her hand rested in his.

"Do you, Clint, take this woman?"

He looked at her and in his eyes lay the answer to all the dreams she had ever dreamed.

"Do you, Holly, take this man?"

Clint slipped a circlet of diamonds on her finger. "With this ring I pledge my love, my heart and all that I am," he said.

She took his hand and placed on his finger a plain gold band. "I, too, pledge my love, my heart and all that I am. For always, Clint."

The Reverend Richardson smiled and covering their joined hands with his, said, "I now pronounce you man and wife." And to Clint he said, "You may kiss your bride."

Clint cupped her face between his hands and kissed her. "My love," he whispered against her lips.

The organ music swelled as they turned and started back down the aisle. Her father's eyes were moist and so were Aunt Lou's. But Rosie was smiling and clapping her hands.

Later that evening, when Holly and Clint left the reception, she made sure that Rosie O'Toole caught her bridal bouquet.

* * * * *

Silhouette®

SPECIAL EDITION

COMING NEXT MONTH

**#979 SUNSHINE AND THE SHADOWMASTER—
Christine Rimmer**
That Special Woman!/The Jones Gang
From the moment they were thrown together, Heather Conley and
Lucas Drury were instantly drawn to each other. Giving in to that
passion made them expectant parents—but would Heather believe in
Lucas's love and stick around for the wedding?

#980 A HOME FOR ADAM—Gina Ferris Wilkins
The Family Way
Dr. Adam Stone never expected to make a house call at his own
secluded vacation cabin. But then the very pregnant Jenny Newcomb
showed on his doorstep. And one baby later, they were on their way to
an instant family!

#981 KISSES AND KIDS—Andrea Edwards
Congratulations!
Confusion over his name unexpectedly placed practical businessman
Patrick Stuart amongst Trisha Stewart and her cute kids. Pat *swore* he
was not the daddy type, but he couldn't resist sweet Trisha and her
brood for long....

#982 JOYRIDE—Patricia Coughlin
Congratulations!
Being thrown together on a cross-country drive was *not* the best way
to find a mate, Cat Bandini soon discovered. Bolton Hunter was her
complete opposite in every way—but with every passing mile, they
couldn't slow down their attraction!

#983 A DATE WITH DR. FRANKENSTEIN—Leanne Banks
Congratulations!
Andie Reynolds had spent her life taking care of others, and she'd
had it. Then sexy Eli Masters moved in next door. The neighbors
were convinced he was some sort of mad scientist. But Andie sensed
he was a single dad in need....

#984 THE AVENGER—Diana Whitney
The Blackthorn Brotherhood
Federal prosecutor Robert Arroya had time for little else but the pursuit
of justice. Then Erica Mallory and her adorable children showed him
how to trust again. But could their love survive a severe test?

ELLEN TANNER MARSH

A FAMILY OF HER OWN
(SE #978, August 1995)

Jussy Waring had been entrusted to care for a little girl, but her lonely heart still longed for that special kind of family she'd only heard about. When Sam Baker came into her and her young niece's life, would she dare hope that her dream could finally come true?

Don't miss A FAMILY OF HER OWN, by Ellen Tanner Marsh, available in August 1995—only from Silhouette Special Edition!

ETM

Tall, dark and...dangerous...

Strangers in the Night

Just in time for the exciting Halloween season, Silhouette brings you three spooky love stories in this fabulous collection. You will love these original stories that combine sensual romance with just a taste of danger. Brought to you by these fabulous authors:

Anne Stuart

Chelsea Quinn Yarbro

Maggie Shayne

Available in October at a store near you.

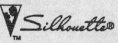

Gina Ferris Wilkins

When their beloved Gram begins to play matchmaker, four cousins find love in the new series by Gina Ferris Wilkins! Meet Adam—and the rest of his family—in Book Three,

A HOME FOR ADAM
(SE #980, September)

Dr. Adam Stone's rest and solitude were interrupted when a very pregnant woman appeared on his doorstep. He helped bring Jenny Newcomb's daughter into the world—and from the moment he looked at mother and child, he wondered if they could provide the love he needed....

Don't miss the warm and wonderful THE FAMILY WAY series! Only from Gina Ferris Wilkins, and Silhouette Special Edition!

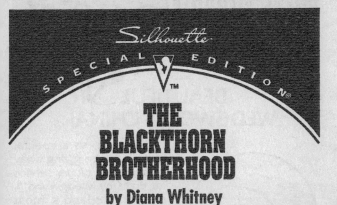

THE BLACKTHORN BROTHERHOOD
by Diana Whitney

Three men bound by a childhood secret are freed through family, friendship...and love.

THE AVENGER (Special Edition #984) When Robert Arroya found a pajama-clad three-year-old in his kitchen, he was more than a little baffled—and smitten with the little imp's mom. Yet Roberto knew a secret that could destroy Erica forever. Could he avenge a wrongdoing and still keep his heart intact?

And watch for **THE REFORMER,** Larkin McKay's story, coming early 1996.

If you missed in the first book—THE ADVENTURER (Special Edition #934, January 1995)—be sure to order your copy today!

PRIZE SURPRISE SWEEPSTAKES!

This month's prize:

BEAUTIFUL WEDGWOOD CHINA!

This month, as a special surprise, we're giving away a bone china dinner service for eight by Wedgwood**, one of England's most prestigious manufacturers!

Think how beautiful your table will look, set with lovely Wedgwood china in the casual Countryware pattern! Each five-piece place setting includes dinner plate, salad plate, soup bowl and cup and saucer.

The facing page contains two Entry Coupons (as does every book you received this shipment). Complete and return *all* the entry coupons; **the more times you enter, the better your chances of winning!**

Then keep your fingers crossed, because you'll find out by September 15, 1995 if you're the winner!

Remember: The more times you enter, the better your chances of winning!*